CW00759055

Diva

Diva

PLAYING FOR HER
BOOK TWO

TESSA VIDAL

Copyright © 2023 by Tessa Vidal

All rights reserved.

No part of this book may be reproduced in any form or by any electronic or mechanical means, including information storage and retrieval systems, without written permission from the author, except for the use of brief quotations in a book review. This is a work of fiction, and any similarities in regards to actual people, events, or settings is coincidental.

For my personal Diva, Montserrat

Prologue

MARIA- TWO YEARS AGO

I HADN'T UTTERED a single word in months, nor had I imbibed a single drop of caffeine or alcohol. No dairy products or heavily spiced foods, just a steady diet of bland food and hot tea with honey. Singing was everything to me, and I'd do whatever it took to preserve my one and only talent, so apart from my work onstage, I was completely silent.

After my voice cracked during a performance at the Met, I limited myself to handwritten notes and text messages, anything to prevent that embarrassment from ever happening again. I'd consulted doctors and specialists, and they all said the same thing: either slow down my performance schedule or stop any unnecessary speech. I chose to keep my mouth shut.

Just last month, I appeared on the cover of Opera Magazine, hailed as the next Beverly Sills. I'd signed a record deal, and my agent had my calendar booked solid for the next year and a half. There was no possible way I could put the brakes on my career. Too many people were depending on me, and with my star on the rise, I needed to work as much as possible.

However, the fear of failing on stage in front of thousands of people never left me.

Now, here I was on one of the grandest stages of all, The Royal Opera House in Covent Garden, with sweat pouring down my sides as I waited for the curtain to rise. The orchestra was tuning their instruments, and the low roar of the crowd taking their seats had subsided. My costume was this ridiculous purple toga, and the rhinestone tiara I wore on my head was digging into my scalp.

"Toi toi toi!" my co-star Adrianna whispered in my ear, the equivalent of "break a leg" for opera singers. I grinned at her, hoping my terror wasn't obvious. She was an emerging star, a Mezzo Soprano with an agile voice and stunning looks that guaranteed her a grand career.

As long as she didn't lose her voice.

Moments later, the scarlet and gold curtain rose, and the performance began.

———

Usually, I lose myself in the music, immersing myself in whatever role I am playing. But tonight, I feared the worst. I loved Baroque Opera and had begged my agent, Clarissa, to find me the perfect role. She had, and to my regret, I found it insanely difficult to perform. It was composed by Handel and was originally meant to be performed by castrati singers. Thankfully, there are no more of them, but even with my role being recast from male to female, the arias were extremely difficult. Every single note had to be sung correctly. It was a battle between substance and style, and the insane number of glissandos and trills was stretching my voice to its limits, even with my complete and utter silence when not singing. Yet, I was doing what I had dreamt of doing my entire life, and if it meant I couldn't speak in order to sing, by God, I'd never talk again.

Instead of period costumes, the stage director had chosen a much more avant-garde production, and I felt pity for my co-stars who performed with little more than a few strategically draped pieces of gauze. Despite the near nudity, the effect was very elegant and refined. We were in the second week of performances, and though I'd had my misgivings, the reviews had been superb, if not the best of my career.

Lyric Soprano Maria Wagner Makes Royal Opera Debit

"...Wagner's voice makes you forget that it was once castrated male singers performing such vocal acrobatics. Her technique and style are sheer perfection, and Maria's star is definitely on the rise!"

But the reviews did nothing to quell my fear. At last night's performance, my voice cracked while hitting the upper limits of my vocal register. The audience hadn't noticed since it was peppered in between a flurry of sixteenth notes, but the conductor had immediately glanced up with a look of concern on his face. After the performance, I went directly to my dressing room and stared at my reflection in the brightly lit mirror, little streaks of black kohl snaking down my cheeks.

"Please, God, don't let that happen again," I mouthed, then swiped at my eyes with the back of my hand.

―――

The fog created by the dry ice wreaked havoc on my vocal cords. Though I'd written a note of complaint to the stage director, he had shrugged it off. The fog appeared purple thanks to the footlights, creating an illusion of singers floating instead of walking across the stage. It was my final aria before being killed by the Queen, the mother of my love interest.

Slowly, I glided up the stage, the spotlight following my

every move. Once there, I waited for the music to begin. The conductor lifted his baton, and the strings began to swirl, followed by the slow thunder of the timpani.

Then, my worst nightmare, the thing I dreaded the most, happened.

I opened my mouth, and only the barest hint of my voice emerged. Forcing myself to continue, I opened my chest and mouth wider, hoping to produce more volume through my vocal cords. But instead of the luscious, natural sound I had been heralded for, all I heard was a croak.

The conductor silenced the orchestra, and the audience glared in my direction. There was nothing I could do to stop the tears, but I didn't want to have thousands of witnesses. I ran off the stage and locked myself in my dressing room. Soon, there was pounding at the door, and I heard a key entering the lock. It had to be the stage director, for he was the only one with the key. The door flew open, banging against the wall, and the elderly man's eyes were filled with pity.

I loathed pity.

"Maria, I'm so sorry. I know a voice specialist who can..."

"Shut up!" I rasped, then snatched a container filled with greasepaint off the scratched wooden counter and threw it at my reflection in the mirror. A long crack splintered it down the middle.

I sank to my knees and sobbed.

CHAPTER

One

CAROLINE

"CAN THIS DAY GET ANY WORSE?" I shivered, glanced at my watch, and wished the bus would hurry up.

By the time I boarded the bus, a cold spring mist covered me. I'd left my umbrella at home, trusting that the weather app on my phone was correct for a change. In theory, it was partly cloudy, with a thirty percent chance of rain. However, the dark clouds swirling overhead as the bus headed north told another story. It matched my mood perfectly, adding another layer of gloom and uncertainty that settled in the pit of my stomach whenever I had to go to my craptastic retail gig.

For the past two months, my co-worker at the cosmetics counter, Andy, had barely spoken to me. I'd been called into my manager's office every week with multiple complaints from him and the other beauty advisors. According to them, I was mowing down my coworkers in my rush to make sales for the *Isabelle Lancray* line that I sold. Essentially they were accusing me of stealing customers. Nothing could be further from the truth. The difference between me and them was that I worked my ass off instead of leaning against the counter gossiping with coworkers. Because of this, I now went to work every day afraid to speak or move, not wanting to provoke their animosity, and my paychecks shrank as a result. I'd barely been able to scrounge enough money to pay the rent on my tiny one-bedroom apartment, and ramen noodles had become a dietary staple.

I worked for Montaldo's department store, and although schlepping lipstick to wealthy older ladies wasn't exactly my dream job, it paid the bills. My degree was in theatrical makeup, but those jobs were insanely hard to find, though I had snagged a few gigs when the occasional Hollywood film was shot in Raleigh. And while makeup counter jobs were fairly easy to come by, none of them could compare to working at Montaldo's. The hours were perfect, and so was the pay. Well, in the beginning the pay was great. Now I made next to nothing thanks to my jealous coworkers. Montaldo's was only open from ten in the morning until seven and were closed on Sundays. It was a luxury retailer, so the typical customer didn't bat an eye shelling out a thousand bucks on a jar of night cream. There was no other retailer in town where I could make such great commission and keep decent hours.

When the doors of the bus opened at my stop, the rain was pouring down. Another perk of my job was the excellent discount on clothing. Unfortunately, the designer threads I was wearing hated water, and I was about to be drenched. I lifted my purse over my head, stepped off the bus, and raced across the parking lot as fast as I could go. By the time I reached the employee entrance, my black wool turtleneck was stuck to my skin, and my loafers were soggy from splashing through puddles. The first person I saw was Andy, looking dry and superior. He smirked in my direction while punching in at the time clock. Since that was the closest thing to a smile I'd had from him in weeks, it instantly filled me with dread.

"Watch your back," Steve whispered as he took my purse. He was in charge of loss prevention, and they held onto our bags while we worked. Since he'd never spoken to me beyond a simple "good morning" before, the drenched hair on the back of my neck tingled. I wanted to ask what he meant, but there was a line forming at the time clock and I couldn't.

My index finger shook as I punched in my ID number. I messed it up and had to do it again, provoking a cascade of groans from the people behind me. It was less than a minute until the store opened, and we were all running behind schedule thanks to the rain. When I turned away from the time clock, I heard a woman's voice whisper, "bitch." My cheeks burned, and I had to stop myself from turning around to see who it was. Instead, I pushed through the double doors and jogged toward my counter, where I saw the cosmetics department manager, Jean, waiting for me, with Andy by her side. I winced as a cramp tore through my stomach.

"Caroline, Kim wants to see you in Human Resources," Jean said, her stare aimed over my shoulder. Andy's eyes never left my face, and the smirk I'd seen earlier was now an ear-to-ear grin. "Now."

"Did she..." I began, but the woman hurried away before I could finish my sentence. Andy ripped open a cardboard box full of stock to put away, that smug grin never leaving his face. My fists clenched, and I had to bite my lower lip to prevent myself from saying something he'd use against me, again. When I turned to leave, I could've sworn I heard him giggle.

I winced and said nothing.

As I crossed the marble floor to the escalator, my eyes instantly went to the Blumarine ripped jeans displayed on the wall next to it. They retailed for $699, and because of the insane amount of feathers and beads embroidered into them, could only be worn once, if at all. They were stunning, and I'd have given anything to be able to afford them. Of course, the practical side of my brain screamed at the utter waste of money. But, the artist in me craved them, and like the visual department had done, I would have framed and hung them up just so I could appreciate their beauty.

This job meant so much to me. I'd never made as much money, and even though I wasn't close to being a rich woman who could shop here, it felt good to say I worked for Montaldo's. Plus, I was an artist. I was surrounded by elegance and beauty, and compared to other retail work, it was cushy, refined, and I wasn't embarrassed to tell dates where I spent thirty-five hours every week.

"Please, Jesus." I crossed myself, and when I got to the third floor I stepped off the escalator and trudged toward human resources.

———

"Caroline, Kim will see you now." I nodded to the receptionist and got to my feet. My legs felt like spaghetti as I walked down the hallway to Kim's office. When I got there, it surprised me to see an unfamiliar face. A statuesque blonde was standing behind Kim, her arms crossed over her chest. Her thin lips were pressed together, and I sensed she was yet another person in the crazy store I shouldn't trust.

"Have a seat." Kim sighed, and after I did, the blonde woman sat next to me and crossed her long legs. We sat in silence for a few moments while Kim drummed her fingers on the desk. Finally, the woman next to me turned and held out her hand for me to shake.

"My name is Theresa Goldman, and I manage human resources for our corporate office."

I had just lifted my hand to shake hers, but it froze in place. Fuck me, but this was Kim's boss, and if she'd made the trip from New York just to see me, it couldn't be good. I shook my head back and forth and briefly took her hand in mine and mumbled, "Nice to meet you."

"Caroline, as you know, the last few months have been rough in our cosmetics department. Unfortunately, you are at the center of the storm," Kim said, steepling her hands under her chin. Then she opened a folder and glanced down. "The first thing we want to do is thank you for your hard work."

My mouth dropped open, and I froze.

"Isabelle Lancray was our lowest-performing cosmetics counter, and you've made it profitable. You are a highly skilled artist and salesman," Kim said, then she pulled a piece of paper from the folder and grimaced. "In fact, you are a top producer in the department. But..." She hesitated, and then the woman next to me, Theresa, interrupted.

"We are very pleased with your performance, but your coworker, Andy Stephens, has accused you of sexual harassment."

"What the... but I'm gay. Andy's gay too. Everyone knows it, like..." My heart hammered in my chest. Jesus fucking Christ, but this was insane. I looked at Kim, who wouldn't meet my gaze, then turned toward Theresa, who did. She shook her head and sighed.

"Yes, we are aware of that, but..." the woman began, but I cut her off.

"You can't seriously believe this. Like, there's no way I'd ever..."

"We would like to believe you, we really would, but

according to our corporate policy, we must investigate the matter, unless..." Kim's voice trailed off, and I noticed her cheeks darkening. I turned to Theresa, who stood up and began to pace behind Kim's desk. Then she stopped and addressed me.

"Sexual harassment is a matter Montaldo's takes very seriously, and we are aware that you are a lesbian, but..."

"Harassment? Why the hell aren't you protecting me from harassment? Do you realize I could take this to court and..." I stammered, noticing Kim wince.

"We're hoping to avoid that. Kim?" Theresa nodded to her, and then Kim slid a piece of paper across the desk and laid a pen on top of it. "The toxicity of the working environment is detrimental to the health of our business. We are prepared to give you three months' severance if you leave your position immediately. You will agree never to seek legal action against Montaldo's and will maintain your silence over this matter."

"This can't be happening," I murmured, then felt tears welling up in my eyes. "What about Andy? Why is it that I'm the only one who..."

"Let us deal with him. Our only concern now is to protect our business, and while we appreciate the hard work you've done while employed here, this has become too big of a problem to ignore." Theresa snatched a Kleenex out of a box on Kim's desk and handed it to me. "I'm truly sorry, but this is the best we can do for you."

My shoulders sagged. I knew it was useless to argue this any further, and all I wanted to do was bolt. The thought of a long drawn-out lawsuit seemed hopeless, and despite the fact that I was losing my job, I also felt a certain sense of relief. I reached for the pen, my fingers shaking as I scrawled my signature on the agreement. When I glanced up, neither woman would look me in the eye. Getting to my feet, I crossed the office and opened the door, unable to speak to either of them.

"Your severance will be deposited into your bank account on Friday. We wish you the best of luck in your future endeavors," Kim said weakly, but I didn't turn around or say anything to acknowledge that she'd spoken. Instead, I straightened my shoulders and walked out, knowing I'd been wronged and helpless to do anything about it.

CHAPTER

Two

CAROLINE

"THANK GOD," I whispered, shutting my laptop and placing it on the coffee table. In doing so, I accidentally knocked an empty pizza box to the floor. True to their word, my severance pay had been deposited into my bank account a week later. I'd never had such a large balance before, and despite the dark cloud hanging over me since my termination, it brought some relief.

"I'd rather have my damn job back," I muttered, rubbing my temples and closing my eyes. For the past few days, I'd been couch-bound, unable to process the events that had unfolded, and worried that Montaldo's would backtrack on the promised compensation. All I could think about was Andy's smug grin as I exited the building after being fired. I intentionally took the service elevator at the rear of the store to avoid anyone witnessing my humiliation. Like a cat toying with its prey, he was waiting when the elevator doors slid open. I rushed past him, yearning for a confrontation that I knew would only worsen matters.

"For Christ's sake, I love women. How could they believe I'd sexually harass Andy of all people?" I repeated for what felt like the hundredth time in the past week. My mind struggled to accept the reality of being betrayed and defeated in the twisted game I never wanted to be a part of. A coworker had sent me a lengthy text detailing Andy's misconduct. Now that I was out of the picture, he'd taken over my position and was managing my former counter. It was clear to everyone that Andy orchestrated my termination to benefit himself financially.

I couldn't comprehend why they'd given credence to Andy's baseless accusations. Why was I the one confined to the couch, surrounded by empty pizza boxes and food-stained takeout containers, while he still had a job? Why was Montaldo's so oblivious?

"At least the rent will be paid," I whispered to the empty walls, then leaned back into the cushions, pulling my knees up to my chest. Tears welled up, blurring my vision.

"Stop it," I muttered, swiping at the tears with the back of my hand. "Have you ever considered that it might be for the best to no longer be in that toxic cosmetics department?"

For the past two months, I'd been plagued by constant stabbing pains in my gut whenever I went to work. Never in my wildest dreams could I have imagined being fired for such a ludicrous accusation as sexual harassment.

"This can't continue."

I straightened my legs, wincing as my muscles stretched out for the first time in hours. Getting to my feet, I padded into the bathroom, switched on the light, and faced my reflection in the mirror. My eyes were red and swollen, and a pimple had emerged on my chin. Greasy black hair clung to my forehead, and there was a smudge of tomato sauce below my lip.

"You were wronged, but now you'll never have to lay eyes on that backstabbing jerk ever again," I whispered, then opened the medicine cabinet and took out my razor and eye drops, only to put the razor back. "It's not like anyone's going to see my legs." I shut the door and stared at myself again, forcing a faint smile. Then I cleared my throat and spoke firmly to the sorrowful face staring back at me.

"You will freshen up, and leave this apartment. I don't care if it's just a walk around the block, but you can't live like this anymore."

———

When I stepped out of the building, the bright sunlight made me squint. It had been days since I last saw it, and I compelled myself to descend the weathered wooden steps onto the brick sidewalk. Initially, I turned towards the park, but then I spun around and walked in the opposite direction. Despite lacking the desire to interact with anyone, I felt the need to be around people. There was a coffee shop on Pearson Street, The Morning Vibe, that I occasionally visited. I'd get a cup of tea and observe what normal, non-depressed people looked like.

I resided downtown in a small apartment building with three other tenants, all NC State students. A greenish-yellow haze of pollen covered the windshields of cars parked on both sides of the street. Spring had officially arrived while I had languished on the couch, feeling sorry for myself. I shrugged off my hoodie and tied it around my waist.

As I reached the end of my block, I spotted a familiar face. Damn it, I didn't want to talk to anyone. I turned back towards the park when her voice rang out.

"Caroline!"

Catrina owned a bar next to the coffee shop I'd been heading towards. We weren't best friends or anything, but we occasionally saw each other at parties held in the neighborhood. As she crossed the street towards me, her tattooed arms spread open for a hug. When she touched me, I flinched. Catrina pulled back, her arms still draped around my neck, and her bright red lips flattened while her eyebrows furrowed.

"What's wrong? You look like someone died."

I bit my lip, not wanting to be a downer. When I opened my mouth to speak, I hesitated, trying to think of something neutral, but instead, the truth slipped out.

"I, um, well, I lost my job."

"Shit. I'm sorry. Did it just happen, or..." she started, but I raised my hand and shook my head.

"Look, I don't want to talk about it. It didn't go well, and I'm still feeling a little raw, if you know what I mean." I averted my eyes and grimaced. "But, thanks for..."

"Where are you headed?" she interrupted. I shrugged my shoulders and opened my mouth, but nothing came out. I felt the now-familiar pressure building up behind my eyes.

"You're coming with me." Catrina grabbed my hand and started pulling me forward. "Sometimes shitty things happen to good people, and you are a good person, Caroline."

"But..."

"I'm not accepting 'no' as an answer," she said in a high-pitched sing-song voice. I wiped at my eyes with my other hand and followed her down the sidewalk.

———

"This round is on the house," Catrina announced, placing a beer and a shot of tequila in front of me. It had been a while since I'd drunk a shot of anything, and when I lifted the glass, the smell almost made me gag. Getting drunk wasn't my usual way of coping with stress; I usually sought solace in junk food and mindless television.

"Bottom's up," I muttered, then downed the shot. It burned

going down, and my eyes watered. Catrina slid a finger bowl of sliced limes in front of me. I took a bite and shuddered. "Jesus, I'd forgotten how terrible tequila tastes."

Catrina chuckled. "Trust me, the second shot goes down a lot smoother than the first."

A customer at the other end of the scratched-up wooden bar waved to get Catrina's attention, and she went to take their order. I sat at the end of the bar next to a worn-out pool table, and I swiveled my head to take in the surroundings. There was a row of booths on the opposite wall, appearing to be in the same condition as the pool table. The exposed brick walls, however, were adorned with artwork, some of which was remarkable. I'd only been here once or twice before and assumed that Catrina was showcasing the work of a local artist.

"Excuse me, young lady, is this seat taken?" A woman's voice drawled. I turned my head to see a large woman with vibrant burgundy hair piled on her head, secured in place with a pair of rainbow-colored chopsticks. It was an odd question, considering it was still early in the afternoon and only a handful of customers were present. I shook my head no, and she took the seat next to me.

"Catrina, darling, Lilith and Bella will be here any minute. Would you mind setting us up with our usual adult beverages?" Loretta Anne requested, and Catrina gave her a thumbs up. Loretta Anne then turned to me. "My name is Loretta Anne."

I noticed two stunning women heading our way. One had vibrant red hair and a wide smile, while the other, with ebony locks, scowled and hastily stuffed her phone into her pocket. Loretta Anne noticed my gaze, turned her head towards them, and waved. Then she leaned in closer to me and whispered, "They're both knockouts. If I were into chicks, I'd be all over them."

For the first time in what felt like forever, I laughed. This eccentric older woman was quite a character. Maybe it was a good thing that Catrina dragged me here after all.

Catrina placed two cocktails in front of the women and a glass of wine for Loretta Anne. Seconds later, she picked up a bottle from behind the bar and raised an eyebrow at me.

"No, I really shouldn't..." I started, but Loretta Anne placed a hand on my thigh. "On second thought, why the hell not," I sighed, wondering how I had gone from being accused of sexual harassment to being bothered by a peculiar older woman.

"Good girl," Loretta Anne remarked, then removed her hand. "What's your name?"

I hesitated for a moment. "Caroline Frank."

"You have stunning eyes," the older woman complimented, leaning closer to me. She might think she's straight, but I had doubts. The redhead next to her laughed.

"Jesus, Loretta Anne, you'll scare the poor girl off," she interjected, extending her hand towards me for a handshake. "My name is Lilith, and you must forgive my friend. She suffers from PBD."

"'PBD?" I had no idea what the hell that was.

"Poor boundary disorder," she cackled, and Loretta Anne swatted her. I shook her hand, and then she pointed to the woman next to her. "This is my wife, Bella. She's normally a little friendlier, but work is driving her nuts right now."

The dark-haired woman gave me a curt nod, then reached into her pocket, pulled out a cell phone, and stood up. "Excuse me." Bella grimaced and walked to the other side of the room, pacing while talking on the phone.

"Did she get the singer?" Loretta Anne asked Lilith, who rolled her eyes.

"Almost," Lilith replied, tilting her head toward Bella, who was now chopping her hand through the air with impatience. "According to Bella, she's being a bit of a prima donna. Who knows? Opera singers are demanding as hell."

"And she's not?" Loretta Anne raised an eyebrow, and both she and Lilith laughed. "I bet whoever the singer is, they've met their match with our conductor."

"You've got to be kidding me!" Bella's voice cut through the air like a knife. I sneaked a glance in her direction as she punched the air, then jammed her phone back into her pocket and stalked over to the bar. "Fucking Maria wants her own personal assistant. Hell, even I don't have one, and I'm the conductor." She drummed her tapered fingers on the bar and glanced in my direction. "She has the right idea. Catrina, pour me a shot."

As Catrina poured, Bella began laughing. "Oh, and Thom Grady put in his notice. Angela will also have to find another makeup artist. We're already stretching our budget, and..."

"Caroline," Catrina interrupted Bella, "is a makeup artist. Aren't you?"

I nodded and opened my mouth to speak, but Bella cut me off.

"Do you know theatrical makeup? You know, special effects and stuff?"

"Yeah, I studied at Tom Savini's school in Pennsylvania. He..."

"Oh, I know who Tom is." Bella's face brightened. "I went to the Curtis Institute in Philadelphia, and some of his students freelanced with our productions. If you studied with him, you're exactly what we're looking for."

For the first time in days, I felt a flicker of hope. I'd only sold makeup at a department store to make ends meet. Theatrical makeup was my passion.

"Are you available? Oh, and just to let you know, I am not in

charge of... wait a minute. This could work." Bella pulled her
phone out of her pocket. "Well, are you?"

"Available?" I pointed at my chest. "Yes, in fact, this is..."
Bella cut me off again.

"I'm not who you would interview with, though I am in
charge of the budget. You'd have to audition with our stage
director. But... let me make a quick phone call." Bella leapt to
her feet and walked outside, where I presumed she was making
the call.

My limbs tingled, and I realized I'd been holding my breath.
I shut my eyes and exhaled. When I opened them again,
Catrina was in front of me, waving the bottle of tequila over my
glass with a smile. I nodded, and she poured. Maybe everything would work out after all, and losing my shitty job was
meant to be.

Loretta Anne and Lilith began talking to me, but all I could
do was mutter yes or no to their questions. I had gone to Tom
Savini's school, hoping that one day I would get to work in
Hollywood. However, I'd fallen in love with a girl from Raleigh
and ended up here. Like so many others before me, once you
lived in Raleigh, it was hard to leave.

The door to the bar swung open, and Bella strolled back in,
her white teeth splitting into a smile.

"You might have solved at least one of my problems." Bella
lifted her drink in my direction and winked. "Let's talk
business."

CHAPTER
Three

MARIA

"REMEMBER EVERYTHING I TAUGHT YOU. Sing from the diaphragm, and if you are uncomfortable with a note, put your foot down and make the conductor alter the passage. You've been incredibly lucky to avoid surgery on your vocal cords, but you might not be so lucky again."

Elise, the vocal coach to whom I owed my career, was right. She had saved my voice, and it had taken almost two years of relearning how to sing to make it happen.

"Are you sure you trust this woman, Bella Lombardi?" Elise paced in front of my bed, making it difficult to pack my suitcase lying on top of it. Her hands twisted around each other compulsively, and I'd swear her nerves were more fraught than mine.

"I don't know her well, but we went to the same school in Philadelphia..."

"The school that taught you how to ruin your voice." She cut me off, then with a sigh, she sat down next to my suitcase and began rearranging my clothes. "Screaming, that's all they taught you. That's all any of those horrible schools teach. They have no respect for the human voice. In fact..."

As Elise continued her diatribe, I thought back to when I'd found her singing school here in Italy. I'd been in the waiting room of a surgeon in London, a specialist who insisted that micro-surgery on my vocal cords was the only path forward. He'd treated countless singers, all famous. He was also very expensive, and since I'd lost my recording contract and my singing gigs, I'd be gambling my life savings in the hopes that once again I could perform. I had nodules on my vocal flaps, and years of oversinging had built up a layer of scar tissue in my throat.

After my very public failure on stage, all of my so-called friends in the music world disappeared. It was like they were afraid that whatever had befallen me would happen to them too, as if vocal cord destruction was contagious. I'd never felt so alone in my life.

Until I met Elise.

Opera Magazine had been lying on the coffee table in the waiting room, so I picked it up to kill time while waiting for my appointment. When I opened it, the first story I saw was about a controversial singing school in Naples, Italy, that claimed to teach a more natural singing style that not only preserved the voice but in some cases healed cases such as mine. A woman named Elise Romano had founded it after her own struggles with her voice. Her method of singing was based on how they trained singers in the nineteenth century when throat injuries were unheard of.

I immediately left the surgeon's office, taking the magazine with me. Ever since that fateful performance at the Royal Opera, my throat had been in agony. I had even received corti-sone injections to soothe the pain and allow me to finish the remainder of my performances, but they had failed. After setting up an appointment with Elise, I packed my bags and gambled that she knew better than the world-famous surgeon who wanted to slice away at my vocal cords with scalpels and lasers.

Elise put my fears to rest, and over the course of two years, she performed a miracle. She restored my voice, and if my ear was to be trusted, improved it immensely. It was a different instrument than it used to be, smoother and richer. Her knowledge of singing and the opera world, in general, profoundly changed me. Thanks to her, I had my career back.

"... you must not allow them to manipulate you into singing music that... are you listening to me?" She glanced up, her dark eyes flashing with impatience, coupled with something else I didn't recognize. Her pale cheeks flushed, and her hands fluttered in her lap.

"I'm sorry, Maestra. I was just thinking about how grateful I am for you and your school. I know I've told you many times how you've given me back my career." I blushed and gave her a little bow. She rose from the bed and placed her hands on my shoulders. Her eyes were damp, and then she stepped into my arms and kissed both my cheeks. Elise then stepped back, and a rare blush stained her cheeks.

"You are my mentor, and I owe you everything," I whispered.

"You've been an excellent pupil, Maria, and, in fact, you are my..." She glanced at her watch, then swiped at her eyes with the back of her hand. "I must be off. My next class will not wait for goodbyes."

Her shoulders stiffened, and then she walked out without looking back or speaking another word.

I had done something most singers of my former stature would never do: signing a two-year contract with a small opera company. Unfortunately, most opera houses did not trust that my voice would hold out, so I had little choice but to accept whatever work I could. My bank account was depleted, and though the contract wasn't as lucrative as I had wished, it would hopefully set me up for bigger and better things.

Two months ago, Elise informed me that my voice was finally ready for work, so I called my agent who immediately put out feelers. It had been humbling, to say the least. Nobody wanted to work with the singer who had lost her voice on stage at the Royal Opera House, and I couldn't blame them one bit. Finally, the North Carolina Opera made an offer and I couldn't say no. Despite being a smaller opera company, they had an excellent reputation, plus I knew the conductor from our years together at The Curtis Institute. It was a small music school in Philadelphia known for excellence, and it was an honor to even be accepted there.

Bella Lombardi had been an intense student, and despite there only being around a hundred pupils at any given time, I only knew her by reputation. Everyone at the school was gifted, but she was known as a temperamental genius who demanded nothing short of perfection from the student musicians she conducted. Of course, this created fear and animosity among the rest of the musicians, but since I studied voice, I didn't have much to do with her.

Bella phoned me herself about the job, and prior to the call, I had braced myself for her volatile temper. She surprised me. Instead of the surliness I had seen from a distance at school, Bella was downright charming. She even said she would try to squeeze a little more money out of the budget and promised me my own personal assistant if I agreed to the full two years.

Without any other offers, I had little choice in the matter. Raleigh, North Carolina, was going to be my new home, whether I liked it or not.

CHAPTER
Four

CAROLINE

"CAN YOU BREATHE OKAY?" I whispered. Catrina gave a slight nod, and then I began sealing the edges of the prosthetic nose with liquid latex on her skin. Catrina turned out to be an awesome friend, agreeing to be the model for my audition. The stage director, Peter Gibb, sat silently on a stool a few feet away, taking notes. He'd been very cool and professional, which set my nerves on edge. I had to focus to keep my fingers from trembling.

The first half of the audition had been a basic stage look using heavy pancake makeup, which I could do in my sleep. Peter surprised me when he asked me to apply a prosthetic nose and then create a bloody wound on Catrina's forehead. The result was wickedly gruesome.

"Oh my God!" Catrina exclaimed when I turned her to face the giant mirror circled with light bulbs. For the first time since we started, Peter smiled, and I felt a kernel of hope.

"That was excellent, Caroline," Peter said, then he took off his heavy, black-framed glasses and examined my work up close. "I can tell you trained with Savini," he murmured, then he put his glasses back on and scribbled on his clipboard. "That's all I need to see. Thank you for coming in, Caroline. I have two more auditions, and then I will make the final decision. You can remove her makeup now."

"No!" Catrina exclaimed, then giggled at her reflection. "I think it will be funny to walk into the bar looking like I got whacked by an ax-murderer." Both Peter and I laughed, then we shook hands, and he left me to clean up.

"I think you got the job, Caroline," Catrina whispered. "This looks amazing." She got up from her stool and took a closer look at herself in the mirror. "Like, wow."

I hated getting my hopes up, but I had to admit I'd done an excellent job with Catrina's makeup. Though Peter kept a poker face throughout the audition, he seemed to be impressed with my work.

"So, are you dating anyone?" Catrina asked.

Well, that came out of left field. I cocked an eyebrow quizzically at her. "Um, no. Why?" I shut my makeup trunk and switched off the lights surrounding the mirror.

"Well, I know a girl who goes to UNC Chapel Hill. She's in the theater department, so I think you two would have a lot in common." Catrina picked up her leather backpack and swung it over her shoulder. I'd dated no one in close to three years, ever since I broke up with Marilyn. Though I was the one who ended it, I still didn't feel ready to date anyone yet.

"I, um, thanks, but no thanks. I broke up with someone a while back, and I'm just not ready to..." I opened the stage door and let her go ahead of me. Not that I was afraid of dating; I just hadn't found a single girl attractive in what seemed like forever. It was like a part of me died when I ended it with Marilyn.

"Well, I'll let you off the hook for now, but you have a lot of things going for you, Caroline. You're gorgeous, and talented too," she pushed the side exit door open. Standing under a tree on the sidewalk facing us was an older woman swiping at her phone. She glanced up, and then her phone clattered to the ground, a look of horror stamped on her face.

"Maybe we should've removed your makeup," I murmured to Catrina, then I bent down and picked up the woman's cell. Thank God the screen hadn't cracked. After apologizing to her, Catrina threw her arm over my shoulder, and we started down the sidewalk toward the parking deck.

"See what I mean? Talented. You're going to get the job, I just know it," Catrina said, and I started to believe it too.

———

"Angela is running ten minutes behind. Is that okay?" A perky blonde receptionist asked. I nodded and felt the butterflies in my stomach flutter around even more. I'd gotten the call for a second interview with Angela Shiflett, who was in charge of human resources for the North Carolina Opera and the Symphony.

I glanced around the waiting area, wishing the interview could be over already. For the first time in what seemed like forever, I felt confident. They wouldn't have called me back for a second interview if they hadn't liked my work.

I drummed my fingers on the arm of the chair and took in my surroundings. The receptionist was typing away on a computer, and across from me was an office surrounded by glass walls with floor-to-ceiling blinds. I was about to pull out my phone to check my email when I noticed one slat of the blinds pulled open. A pair of dark brown eyes appeared. Our eyes locked, and then the blind snapped shut. I swallowed, wondering if it was Angela who had been sneaking a peek in my direction.

My palms were sweating, and I rubbed them on my knees. Then I noticed a tall, thin woman with dark hair pulled back into a severe bun striding toward me with her hand out.

"Caroline Frank?" I stood and shook her hand, hoping she didn't notice the dampness. "I'm Angela Shiflett. I've heard wonderful things about you from both Bella and Peter. Follow me." She spun around and walked past the glass-walled office. Whoever had been peeking at me hadn't been her.

Angela's office wasn't very large, and the bright yellow walls made the room seem bigger than it was. They were covered in framed posters from past performances of the Symphony and Opera. She waved me toward a wooden chair in front of her desk.

"So, according to Peter, you did a splendid job with your audition." She began, then she leaned back in her chair and inhaled. "But he's decided to hire someone else for the makeup designer position."

My stomach dropped, and I struggled to keep my face neutral. Why on earth had they called me back for a second interview? Couldn't they have told me this over the phone?

The woman seemed to read my mind and began to speak in low, modulated tones. "The reason we had you come in today was to make you an offer for a different position, one that would still utilize your talents with makeup artistry, plus... more." She steepled her hands under her chin and smiled.

I struggled to find the right words to respond but only managed a feeble, "Okay."

"Are you a fan of opera?" She asked. I licked my lips, wondering how to be diplomatic while still being truthful.

"I have a passing knowledge of it, but I enjoy all sorts of music." I didn't want to admit that I knew next to nothing about it. When I thought of opera, all I could picture was the stereotypical woman wearing a helmet with huge horns wailing dramatically onstage.

"The North Carolina Opera has been afforded an incredible opportunity to work with a talented soprano by the name of Maria Wagner. Have you heard of her?" She tilted her head.

"Yes," I stated, though I didn't know who she was. I'd heard the name from Bella while sitting at the bar with her, her wife, and that strange woman Loretta Anne. It wasn't really a lie.

"Maria's an immensely talented singer who has performed in the best opera houses around the globe. Maria has signed a two-year contract with the North Carolina Opera, and she needs a personal assistant. The position includes applying her stage makeup, and you would also be in charge of her wardrobe and costume changes." She lifted an eyebrow and waited for me to respond. While this wasn't what I wanted to do, it would get my foot in the door and hopefully lead to better things. Plus, the thought of going back to another retail job made my blood run cold.

"I've worked in the theater, so I definitely can do the job." I forced myself to meet her gaze and speak without sounding too disappointed. "Though I must confess that I've never been a personal assistant before."

"I've prepared a job description for you." She opened a folder and slid a few sheets of paper across the desk to me. I picked it up, and Angela resumed talking. "As you can see, it's a very detail-oriented position, and you will be our very first PA at the North Carolina Opera. We're making a huge investment in Maria Wagner, and your job will be to take care of her and her needs so she can focus solely on what she does best: singing. An important part of your job will be taking care of her social media presence. If you flip to page three, you'll see what that entails. You will coordinate with the PR department to make sure her social media messages are always on point."

I had a Twitter and Facebook account, so I couldn't imagine it being all that hard. Actually, it sounded easy, though for some reason Angela was making it sound difficult.

"It's a demanding job, and you must understand that your life will revolve around Maria. While we know you're not a mind reader, you must learn to anticipate her every need. You will also travel with Maria to performances related to the North Carolina Opera. Does this sound like a position you'd enjoy?" Her eye twitched, which struck me as odd, almost as if she expected me to say no. Since I never wanted to work behind a makeup counter again, taking the job was an easy decision. But I needed to see if it paid well enough to make it worth my while.

"What is the salary?" I gulped, always nervous to bring up the topic of money. Angela smiled, then pulled another sheet of paper out of the folder and slid it across the desk.

Oh my freaking God.

This was far more than I made working in retail. Hell, I think it paid better than the makeup designer job I'd just been turned down for.

"Yes, I would love to be Maria Wagner's personal assistant," I blurted, then mentally kicked myself for sounding too eager.

Angela's lips slid open. "As you can see, the remuneration is excellent. Let me make this perfectly clear. For the next two years, you will be on call twenty-four hours a day, seven days a week. If your performance meets expectations, I'm sure we'll have more work for you after Maria's contract is up." Then she slid another document across the desk to me. "This is a Non-Disclosure Agreement. By signing it, you guarantee your silence while working with Maria. It applies not only for the length of your employment but afterward too."

I flipped through the pages and felt my heart thump in my

chest. What the hell was I getting myself into? The money was fabulous, but was it worth giving up my entire life?

"Why do I have to sign this?" I asked, and my knee hit her desk with a thump. Angela's eyes glanced away from mine. "Because of the intimate nature of your work. This position involves you in almost all aspects of Maria's life, which means you must keep any private information about her out of the public eye. Discretion is a must, and it's required that you sign the NDA."

What did I have to lose? It wasn't like she was Madonna or Beyoncé, and I couldn't imagine what she'd ever do that would be that interesting to the public. Plus, if I ended up hating the job, I could always find something else.

"May I have a pen?"

———

The receptionist, who introduced herself as Penny, walked me to an empty office where I was to fill out a stack of paperwork. Ten minutes later, she poked her head in the door. "Ms. Lombardi would like a moment with you."

It took me a second to realize it was Bella. I got to my feet and followed her down the hall until we were in front of the glass-walled office. "She's expecting you, just give a little knock." Penny smiled then sat behind her desk. The blinds were now open, so I peered through the glass before knocking. Bella was pacing the length of the room, and then she caught me staring. She waved, then showed me into her office.

"Have a seat." Bella pointed to a small leather loveseat across from her desk. "So, Angela told me the good news. I know you had your heart set on the makeup designer position, but I think you'll do an excellent job working with Maria."

"I certainly hope so. Though I..."

"The reason I brought you here was to speak candidly about your new job." Bella interrupted, then leaned back in her chair and sighed. "The North Carolina Opera is the fifteenth largest opera company in the United States. My goal is to break into the top ten, and the only way to do it is with star power. We've invested a substantial portion of our budget in procuring Maria, and in you."

I lifted my chin, hoping I looked more confident than I felt.

"This past year, both the Met and The National Opera laid off hundreds of employees and slashed their budgets. We're one of the few opera companies in the US that is profitable." Bella grinned, but then her lips pressed together, and she pointed at me. "Your job is to make Maria Wagner happy. She had some bad luck two years ago with her voice, and we were one of the only opera houses willing to take a risk on her, which is how we could afford... anyway, Maria is your job. If she wants anything, it is your responsibility to make it happen, no matter how ludicrous the demand. Do you understand what I'm saying?"

"Yes, ma'am." My voice trembled, and I hoped she hadn't noticed. What the fuck was I getting myself into?

"Please, call me Bella. Only Penny says ma'am or calls me by my last name. Can't break her of the habit." Bella stood, walked to the door, and placed her manicured fingers on the doorknob. Apparently, our little talk was over, so I followed her. "You will see me almost as much as Maria. Rehearsals begin on Monday, so you have four days to enjoy your life. Stay out until dawn, or take a trip to the beach or the mountains. Do whatever you love to do the most because starting next week, your life belongs to Maria Wagner."

CHAPTER
Five

CAROLINE

I GAVE serious thought to taking a weekend trip to the Outer Banks and renting an inexpensive hotel room on the beach. It was the off-season, so it wouldn't be too pricey. However, then I thought about the uncertainties that came with a new job. What if I didn't like it, or if the opera singer hated me? Though I had a healthy bank balance due to the generous severance given to me by my old job, I knew I'd feel safer if I could hold on to it as long as possible. I'd never had an emergency fund before, and just knowing the money was there did a lot to calm my nerves.

Instead of the beach, I prepared myself for the long hours of the new job. I cleaned the apartment from top to bottom, demolished the pile of dirty clothes in my closet, and even went jogging along the river. When I returned home exhausted from the run, I eyed the pizza boxes and empty potato chip bags littering the coffee table. I wanted to revamp my junk food eating habits. The healthier I was, the better I could cope with long hours and temperamental musicians. Plus, a complete change of diet was long overdue. I cleaned out my fridge and pantry of all the junk, putting it in a box to give to the homeless shelter downtown. Then I took an Uber to the health food store in Cary, the one I'd never been able to afford, and stocked up.

"Goodbye junk, hello veggies," I said as I eyed the little plastic box of stringy alfalfa sprouts and the assorted greens and brightly colored fruits. "I solemnly vow that you won't rot in the crisper." I crossed myself, then shut the door to the fridge. After that, I began making my favorite comfort food, which not only tasted great but also cured me of childhood colds and the flu: homemade chicken soup made from my mom's recipe. The only deviation I made was to add dumplings, a southern touch my Yankee mom didn't know about.

Since I was to be on call for my job around the clock, I was doubling the recipe and freezing most of it to eat later. Cooking was my favorite way to relax, and since I was always stressed out, it surprised me that I didn't do it more often.

"You'd lose your gut if you'd lay off the pizza," I patted myself on the tummy, then grabbed a knife and began preparing the ingredients.

Half an hour later, it was simmering on the stove, and since it took a few hours to cook, I popped some low-fat popcorn in the microwave, poured a glass of organic red wine, and settled on the couch to watch a movie. I had no idea what to watch, so I scrolled through Netflix until a movie I'd never seen before caught my eye. It was "The Devil Wears Prada," and if I recalled correctly, it was about a personal assistant.

"I can't believe I've never watched this before," I muttered, then put my feet up on the coffee table and clicked the remote. "Ooh, Anne Hathaway is hot."

———

By the time the final credits rolled, my stomach was in knots. The insane demands of Meryl Streep's character had terrorized the personal assistant, and I wondered if I was making a huge mistake.

"Jesus, if Maria Wagner is anything like Miranda Priestly, I'll be lucky to last a week." I sighed, then resisted the urge to pour myself another glass of wine. Instead, I checked on the soup, got my laptop out of the bedroom, and stalked my future boss online.

"Speaking of hot, Maria's gorgeous." There were quite a few pictures of her, mostly of Maria onstage in a variety of costumes. There was one picture of her offstage, wearing an expensive gown with her arm around a woman with long, dark hair. Wagner had been a promising star, singing in huge opera houses around the globe, only to lose her voice while performing onstage. According to Wikipedia, she'd been born in Montreal but grew up in Hartford, Connecticut. Then she'd gone to some famous music school in Philadelphia, and beyond that, there wasn't much else to read. Apparently, she kept her private life just that, private.

"Well, if you are anything like Meryl Streep's character, I'm history." Then I clicked onto the Nordstrom website and filled out an online application for another sucky makeup artist position.

Just in case.

———

"Thank you for coming," Angela said with a smile, then gestured for me to sit. It was as if she doubted I would actually show up. "Here's a laptop and a phone. You will also use this credit card for all purchases made for Maria, which she reimburses us for. In the folder is a list of passwords so you can access the North Carolina Opera social media accounts, and a list of rules Maria wants you to follow."

I glanced at the small pile perched in front of me on her desk, my mind immediately latching onto Maria's rules.

"Maria will be here later this morning. Do you have any questions I can answer before she arrives?" Angela asked, and I noticed that the color of her makeup didn't match her neck. It surprised me since, other than that, she was very chic. Her hair was in a bun, which I soon learned was her everyday look, and she had a strand of classic pearls around her thin, elegant neck, complete with matching earrings.

"No, I can't wait to meet her."

Angela stood and gestured for me to follow her. "Let me show you to your office."

I grabbed the stuff off the desk, stuffed it all in a pricey leather bag I'd splurged on, and followed her to the elevator. We went up to the seventh floor, and the door opened onto a large room filled with cubicles. There were about thirty bored-looking people with headsets on, all talking at once.

"This is our telemarketing department. They make a huge difference with our fundraising." She waved in their direction and then led me down a long corridor.

At the end of the hallway, she opened a door and stepped back. The office was the size of a broom closet, and I could see why she hadn't entered with me. The walls were beige and bare, and the scratched-up metal desk had seen better days.

"Why don't you familiarize yourself with the social media accounts? Oh, and the PR department is located on the sixth floor directly underneath us. When you get a chance, run down and introduce yourself. We're planning an intense campaign around Maria, and you'll play a big role. Inside the folder I gave you is a list of all the department extensions, including mine. Give me a ring if you have questions."

When the door shut behind her, I sank into the ancient wooden chair behind the desk and wished I had at least a tiny window for some natural light. The fluorescent tubes on the ceiling made a buzzing sound and hurt my eyes, and I wondered if they had gotten the furniture at a thrift store. "You are definitely starting at the bottom. Well, maybe not," I mumbled, thinking of the poor telemarketers down the hall.

I opened the folder and glanced over the rules. There was nothing out of the ordinary, mostly just to be available at all times and to keep my mouth shut about anything seen or heard.

"Well, she doesn't seem as bad as Miranda Priestly," I muttered, then I opened the laptop and started looking over the Twitter and Facebook accounts. It surprised me that Wagner didn't have her own personal social media accounts, and I wondered if I'd be setting them up for her.

The cell phone Angela gave me rang, startling me, and when I picked it up, it rang again, and I dropped it. I scrambled to answer it before it could ring again.

"Caroline Frank," I said breathlessly, hoping I sounded marginally professional.

"She's here, Maria's here." Angela's voice sounded hurried. "Come down to Bella's office, now." She disconnected the call.

"Well, this is it. Time to meet your fate." I said to the blank walls, my heart pounding.

———

The hallway outside Bella's office was packed. The only people I recognized were Bella, her wife Lilith, and Angela. I assumed everyone else was a musician or singer. Turned out I was wrong.

"Remember their faces," Angela whispered in my ear. "Some of them are reporters. Never talk to them."

I still couldn't believe this much fuss was being made over

an opera singer, then kicked myself for not listening to any of the YouTube videos of Maria performing. She must be an amazing singer to garner this kind of attention.

"What does Maria think of Raleigh?" a man's voice called out.

"How's your voice, Maria?" another person shouted.

"Thank you, but this is Maria's first day and we have a busy agenda. Our publicity department will be in touch with you in the next couple of days to set up interviews," Bella announced. Then the crowd of reporters parted, and I laid eyes on Maria Wagner, promptly forgetting how to breathe.

She was nothing short of breathtaking, commanding the attention of all those present. A vision of elegance and grace, she stood tall, her statuesque figure casting a spell on everyone present.

Her lithe form was clothed in a gown of flowing silk, hugging her every curve with a gentle caress. The fabric clung to her as if it knew it had the honor of adorning a goddess. The dress, a masterpiece of design, accentuated her elegant neck, trailing down to showcase her slender waist before cascading into a gentle swirl of fabric around her shapely hips.

Maria's lustrous mane of chestnut waves cascaded down her back, framing a face that belonged to the realm of dreams. Perfectly symmetrical features, delicate and yet imbued with a captivating allure, adorned her visage. Her sparkling emerald eyes, as if holding the secrets of the universe, gleamed with a mischievous twinkle, hinting at a playful spirit beneath her composed exterior.

Maria Wagner was captivating, and possibly the most elegant woman I'd ever laid eyes on.

"Step into my office," Bella said to Maria as the crowd thinned out. Then she gestured for me and a man I didn't know to join them. My feet felt like they were encased in concrete, and I feared I would trip. I shook my head back and forth a couple of times and willed myself forward. A mahogany table with four high-backed chairs had been placed in the center of Bella's office, the leather loveseat now against the wall. Bella gestured for us to sit.

"Now that we're alone, I just want to say how good it is to see you again, Maria. It's been what, fifteen years or so?" Bella asked. Maria smiled and nodded. "Today we'll go over our schedule for the season, the publicity we'll be doing, and of course, the inevitable fundraising drive that you will play a role in." Again, Maria nodded and said nothing.

"This is my assistant conductor, Phillip Capone." Bella gestured toward a short, middle-aged man standing next to her. "And this is your personal assistant, Caroline Frank."

Maria grinned and extended her hand for me to shake. "Nice to meet you," I said, her grip firm and surprisingly calloused. I wondered if she could feel my pulse throbbing in my wrist, then realized that I was holding my breath along with her hand. I dropped it and felt my ears grow hot.

"Caroline, if you don't mind, please take notes, and when we are done, email all of us a copy," Bella said. So, I pulled out my laptop and sneaked a quick glance at Maria, then tore my eyes away before she caught me.

Focus, Caroline, focus.

Phillip tapped me on the shoulder and handed me a pen, nodding in Maria's direction.

Maria's fingers brushed mine as she took the pen, and then she pulled a small notebook out of her orange Birkin bag. Jesus, I could probably live for a year on the price of that purse. The veins on her neck corded as she scribbled something down, then tore out the paper and handed it to me.

A tall glass of warm, not hot water.

"Warm water? Okay." I pushed my chair back and rose from the table.

"While you're in the break room, would you please bring us a carafe of coffee?" Bella asked, and of course, I nodded and smiled. Normally, this wouldn't be a problem, but I had no idea where the break room was. Then I remembered that Bella's secretary was probably at her desk and could point me in the right direction.

As I stepped out of Bella's office, it struck me that Maria hadn't spoken once. My nerves were so on edge I hadn't even thought it odd that she was writing notes instead of talking. Was this my fate for the next two years? To work with a woman who couldn't even be bothered to open her mouth except to sing? But then I pictured Maria's perfect oval face and curves.

"I can make this work," I sighed, then hurried off to find the break room.

CHAPTER
Six

MARIA

MY FORMER CLASSMATE, Bella Lombardi, seemed genuinely glad to see me. Though we didn't know each other well, she'd always been professional with me at the Curtis Institute. I could tell Bella was attempting to put me at ease, but her courteousness was having the opposite effect.

I was terrified.

Before I arrived today, I had sent Bella an email letting her know that I wasn't speaking to help preserve my voice. It was better for her to think that than to know the reality: I was scared out of my mind that I would fail her, and worse yet, I would ruin what I had left of my tattered career.

One thing I learned after losing my voice was that relying on notes and electronic communication allowed me to control my words better. Instead of blurting out the first thing that came to mind, writing it down forced me to choose my words with care. The truth was, my voice was in the best shape of my life. I had no problems talking, but Bella didn't need to know that.

"Here you go," my new assistant mumbled as she placed a

glass of water in front of me. Her fingers trembled slightly, and then, as she set a tray on the table, one of the coffee mugs fell off and her pale cheeks flushed. "Oops," she muttered, placing the mug next to her laptop before falling back into her seat.

"Let's look at the schedule for the upcoming season first," Bella said as she poured herself a cup of coffee, ignoring the packets of sugar and creamer next to the carafe. I loved the smell of coffee, but caffeine was a big no-no for my throat. I sipped water, grateful that my assistant had gotten the temperature perfect on the first try—neither too hot nor cold. I opened the folder in front of me and saw a packed schedule. What took me by surprise were the first round of performances. They had a set of shows coming up that had never been discussed with me or my agent. I pulled my notebook out and scribbled out a question, handing it to my assistant, and then pointed to Lombardi. Her vivid eyes met mine, and that's when I remembered her name: Caroline.

Lombardi took the paper from Caroline and grimaced. "We sent your people notice about this showcase two weeks ago. It's only five shows featuring select arias from the upcoming season—just you, a pianist, and strings." Bella stood and walked over to her desk, retrieving her laptop. She opened it, typed something, and handed it to Caroline, who then handed it to me.

Lombardi was correct. The fault lay with my agent, who had never told me about these performances. I handed the laptop back and scribbled another note.

I'm sorry. My agent didn't inform me of this. I will gladly do the showcase, but I don't want to strain my voice. I want input on the arias to be sung.

Lombardi smiled. "Thank you, and of course, you'll have input on the arias. The point of the shows is to introduce our star performer to the public and generate excitement for the upcoming season. There will be two shows here in Raleigh, one in Greensboro, and two in Charlotte at the Belk theater. That show is the most important, so we scheduled those last. We want to get a good write-up in the newspapers. Plus..."

As Lombardi continued speaking, I shifted in my seat so I could observe Caroline out of the corner of my eye. Her fingers flew over the keys, trying to keep up with what was being said, while her full lips pressed together with determination. The woman was beautiful, with black hair cut short, pale skin, and insanely long black eyelashes. Caroline glanced in my direction, catching me observing her. I shrugged my shoulders and smiled, turning my attention back to Lombardi.

"...Cosi fan Tutte always does well for us, but we also want to stretch our artistic chops a bit by performing a new opera. It's for next season, but I would love for you to look over it. It's, well, I'm the composer." Lombardi's cheeks darkened, and she eyed me expectantly. This didn't shock me in the slightest, since her reputation not only at school but professionally preceded her. I grinned and wrote a note for Caroline to hand to her.

You're very gifted, and it would be an honor to work with you on an original opera you've composed.

"Excellent!" Lombardi clapped her hands together, then closed her folder and laptop and rose from her chair. "Let's take an hour for lunch and then begin rehearsals. It will be just you, me, Peter, and the piano."

I held a finger up, wrote in my pad, and handed it to Bella.

Will Caroline be needed for rehearsal?

"No, but she can be there if you..." Bella began, but I held up my hand and wrote another note and passed it to Caroline. She started to hand it to Lombardi, but I laid my hand on her arm and nodded at her. Caroline scanned the note, then spoke. Aside from a brief greeting, I hadn't really heard her speak yet.

Caroline's voice was surprisingly smooth, a contralto, though it trembled just the slightest bit.

"Ms. Wagner wants me to go to her apartment and unpack her library, plus supervise a furniture delivery."

"That's not a problem at all," Bella shrugged. "We have your cell phone number, Caroline, so if we need you, we'll call." Then she and the assistant conductor, whose name I couldn't remember, walked out of the office.

Caroline closed her laptop and packed it away in a leather bag. I quickly wrote down my address and provided more specific instructions about what needed to be done. Then I stood up and walked to the door, glancing into the hallway to ensure it was clear. The conductor and her assistant were at the receptionist's desk down the hall. I closed the door for a moment and turned to the young woman.

"Please, from now on, call me Maria. Oh, and don't tell them..." I tilted my head toward the door. "...that you heard me speak."

CHAPTER
Seven

CAROLINE

AS THE UBER eased down the street to the address Maria had given me, I couldn't stop thinking about three things. First, why was Maria pretending that she couldn't or wouldn't talk to Bella? Second, why had she confided that little tidbit to me? And third, that my new boss provoked serious feelings in me.

Before Maria left for lunch, she pressed a key into my palm and closed my fingers around it, then held my hand for a beat too long. When she did that, I held my breath and realized my panties were in danger of drowning.

"The key to my apartment is for you to keep. I'm prepared to trust you with my life, and I hope it will be rewarding for both of us," Maria murmured, her dark magnetic eyes locking with mine. My heart hammered in my chest, and my knees felt like spaghetti. Then she let go of my hand, turned, and walked out. As soon as the door shut, I fell into a chair and put my face in my hands, wondering if I could handle being so close to the woman while maintaining my composure. After being fired for sexual harassment, and despite the false nature of those charges, I was determined to be strictly professional with my new boss.

"We're here," the driver said, his tone sharp. I thought he had already said it once and was trying to get me out of his car so he could pick up another ride.

"Oh, sorry," I breathed and exited the car, then peered up at the tall apartment building. It was the only high-rise in Oakwood, and I could see it from my bedroom window. It was on the edge of the neighborhood, with spectacular views of downtown Raleigh. My neighbors hated the building because it was so new, plus it didn't fit in with the vibe of the neighborhood, which was filled with old homes, brick side-walks, and an amateur guitarist or bongo player on every porch. Oh, and the occasional bong too, if my sense of smell was accurate.

It surprised me that Maria chose to live in Oakwood. Most wealthy people set up housekeeping in the country or near the country club. But then again, Maria wasn't from here, so she probably didn't know any better.

There was a flat metal rectangle next to the entrance, which I assumed was where I was supposed to punch in the code Maria had written down. After fumbling through my bag, I pulled out the note and punched in the numbers. Usually, you would hear a click after punching in a code on security doors, but I heard nothing, and when I tried to open it, nothing happened. I punched in the code again, careful to get each digit correct, but the door wouldn't budge.

"Damn it," I groaned, resting my forehead against the glass door. Making a good impression was important, and inter-rupting Maria on my first day wasn't the way to do it. "Maria wrote it down wrong." I pulled out my phone, ready to make a call, but then realized Maria was at lunch with Bella and that other guy, unable to speak freely. So, I quickly typed out a text and was about to hit send when I heard a familiar voice behind me.

"Hey, what are you doing here, Caroline?"

I spun around and saw Catrina's bright red lips spread across her cheeks. Her dark hair fluttered in the cool spring breeze.

"Oh, thank goodness it's you." I hugged her. "You live here, right?"

She nodded.

"I need to get inside, but my boss gave me the wrong code." I showed her the piece of paper Maria had written the code on.

"She forgot to write down the pound sign, that's all." Catrina entered the code and added the pound sign at the end. "There you go. So, why does Bella want you here? She and Lilith don't live in the building anymore." She held the door open, and I entered with her following closely.

"Well, I didn't get the makeup artist job. Instead, I'm working as a personal assistant for her star singer, Maria Wagner. Apparently, she lives here and..."

"Oh my God, you mean that stunning woman who moved into Frank's old penthouse?"

I wasn't familiar with Frank, but I certainly agreed with Catrina about my sexy boss.

"Who's Frank?" I asked, curious.

"Frank's my brother. He owns the building, and when he and Spencer got married, they decided to buy a house. Frank's been trying to rent out the penthouse ever since." Catrina pressed the up button on the elevator. "By the way, what's the singer's story?" she asked, raising an eyebrow.

"What do you mean?" I replied. I'd only just met Maria, so I didn't know any more about her than Catrina did.

"Well... does she play for your team or mine?" Catrina ran her fingers through her hair, and the elevator doors slid open.

It was mirror lined, and our reflections bounced around the small space. Catrina pressed the buttons for the fifth floor and the penthouse. "So?"

"Are you asking if she's gay or not? Um, I've just met Maria. I'm not sure, but I think she's straight," I answered, recalling that when she held my hand earlier, I briefly thought she might be interested in women. Who knows? It didn't matter since she was off-limits. Catrina's eyes widened, and she chuckled.

"I've never been with a woman before, but she's so gorgeous that I'd make an exception for her." She bit her lower lip, and a flush crept up her neck.

The doors slid open on the fifth floor, and Catrina stepped halfway out and leaned against the side to keep them from shutting. "I'm in 5B if you need anything. Just text me. Do you have my number?" I shook my head no and handed her my phone. After she finished entering her number, she gave me a peck on the cheek. "If you get lucky with your new boss, I want to know everything!"

When I arrived at Maria's floor, the elevator opened onto a small hallway with only one door. I took the key out of my pocket, and as the door opened, I froze.

"Wow," I whispered, mesmerized by the sunlight pouring in from the floor-to-ceiling glass windows on the other side of the living room, leading to a balcony. The parquet wooden floors were polished to a high shine, the walls painted a muted heather. Aside from a few unopened boxes, the living room appeared empty. I closed the door and made my way across the room towards the balcony doors, stepping outside.

"This is... unreal," I breathed, taking in the breathtaking sights. The balcony stretched along the entire length of the building. As I reached the edge, vertigo shot through me, causing me to tightly grip the handrail. It surprised me since I wasn't normally afraid of heights. Glancing down, I noticed how small people appeared as they walked through downtown. The skyline looked stunning from this elevation, offering a completely different experience than from ground level.

"This beats the view from my windows by a mile," I sighed, thinking about the small patch of brick wall my bathroom window showed. "Now this is living."

Reluctantly, I walked back inside, only to feel the cell phone that the Symphony had given me buzzing in my pocket. It was the furniture delivery men, informing me that they were downstairs and needed to be let inside.

"Okay, Caroline. It's time to get your act together."

———

"Damn it, Maria, why didn't you give me a floor plan?" I bitched, having to guess where each piece of furniture went. It was my first day of work, and I had no clue what I was doing. Without instructions, I worried that I had gotten everything wrong. I fell back onto the sleek black leather couch I had placed in the living room, exhausted. The delivery men I'd let in earlier were only the first of three deliveries. The first two were from furniture stores, while the third was a moving company dropping off stuff Maria had in storage.

Obviously, the kitchen, living room, and bathrooms (four!) were easy to identify. So was Maria's bedroom, which had a king-sized mattress on the floor. Thank goodness the delivery men had been instructed to put the bed frame together because I couldn't have managed that on my own.

Maria seemed to appreciate simplicity when it came to decorating. If she'd been some kind of wealthy hoarder, I would've lost my mind. Well, she hoarded books, but I wouldn't hold that against her. The library was an easy room to find since it had built-in mahogany bookcases with stacks of boxes in front of them. There were piles of boxes in the bedrooms (five!) to organize, but I needed to know which rooms they were supposed to go in.

"Must be nice," I murmured, then heard a key in the front door and got to my feet. It swung open, and Maria stood in the doorway for a moment, looking around. When she saw me, she grinned, shut the door, and strolled over, looking more and more like a goddess with each step.

Breathe, Caroline, breathe.

"So, it looks like you were kept busy today," Maria said in a low, even voice. "I hope things went well." She laid her expensive purse on the table in front of me. Her dress was so elegant, the fabric cascading down her body, draped in all the right places, highlighting her perfect silhouette. This woman was so out of my league, but it was like my hormones had gone into overdrive.

My mouth opened to reply, but she spun around and started walking down the hallway toward her bedroom, calling over her shoulder, "I'll be right back." Once I heard her bedroom door shut, I groaned and shut my eyes.

"C'mon, Caroline, act professional for Christ's sake," I murmured, then closed my eyes for a moment and imagined Sister Mary Eunice, my high school biology teacher, slapping a ruler against the palm of her hand. After a minute, I felt my arousal dwindle down until I heard Maria's voice.

"Are you okay?"

"Oh, sorry, um, I was just... picturing what this place will look like once you've, you know, put it together," I stammered, taking in the sight of my boss who was now wearing a plain white t-shirt, pink sweatpants, and sneakers. My mouth went dry, and blood rushed to my cheeks.

"It's going to be fabulous. I'm not used to such a large place. I've spent most of my career living in hotel rooms." She laid her hand on my shoulder, and I noticed she kept her nails short with a clear coat of lacquer. "You did a great job today, Caroline. Let's call it a night. Go home and get some rest because we have a lot of work to do tomorrow."

"Um, sure, that sounds great," I breathed, then remembered my leather bag was on the kitchen counter. "My things are in the kitchen," I said while Maria walked to the front door and waited for me to retrieve it. When I met her in the hallway outside her apartment, she surprised me by getting into the elevator.

"Going to work out in the gym downstairs," she said as the doors slid shut. "Meet me tomorrow morning at nine here. Rehearsals don't start until one, but I'll need help moving things around and unpacking. Oh, and don't wear anything you don't mind getting dirty. We'll be working up a sweat."

"Yes, ma'am," I murmured, trying not to imagine her covered in a slick sheen of perspiration. Then the doors opened into the lobby. Maria gestured for me to exit first, and as I walked forward, she grabbed my shoulder, the heat of her fingers burning through the fabric of my shirt.

"Drop the *ma'am*. It's Maria. Now get some rest because I'll be giving you a workout tomorrow."

CHAPTER

Eight

CAROLINE

"NO, NOT YET." I groaned into my pillow as the alarm on the phone screeched. It had taken most of the night to fall asleep, and I was exhausted. Well, most of me was. I'd been grinding into the mattress in my sleep.

"Stop it." I pushed down one more time, then rolled over and snatched the phone from the nightstand. After turning off the noisemaker, I sank back into my pillows and threw the sheets over my head. A split second later my fingers were inching under my panties, and I forced myself to pull them out.

Normally I loved to get myself off. It hurt no one, felt amazing, and best of all it was free. But every time I'd shut my eyes to imagine some anonymous vixen, images of Maria invaded my brain. So, I watched porn instead. And wouldn't you know it, but the first woman that caught my eye was a dead ringer for my new boss. That's when I'd shut my laptop, put my robe back on and tried to blot out the frustration via cooking shows. That worked for an hour, but as soon as I slid under the sheets to go to sleep my imagination kicked into overdrive, and all I could think about was Maria. Instead, I'd taken some melatonin and hoped it would knock me out.

All I wanted to do now was get off, and I wondered if I would make it through an entire day of being around Maria without spontaneously combusting from pent-up sexual desire. I forced myself to think of angry nuns, moaned with despair, then threw the sheets back and stared at the ceiling.

"You are a fucking hot mess, Caroline." I swung my legs over the side of the bed and rubbed the sleep from my eyes. "Maria is my boss. Imagine that she's a sexless plastic doll with nothing between her legs. She doesn't want me and never will."

Now if only I could make myself believe it.

———

A text from Maria hit my phone while I was waiting for the elevator in the lobby of her apartment building.

> Door is open- come in

When the elevator doors slid open, an older woman and two guys my age got off, all smiles. When the doors shut behind me I was the only person on it, and as it climbed up the floors I stared at my reflection in the mirrored walls and mouthed, "Be professional" over and over until the doors slid open in front of Maria's apartment. Then I crossed myself, though I wasn't a believer anymore, walked across the hall and opened the door. My mouth fell open at the sight before me. Standing on the balcony, taking in the morning view was Maria, wearing nothing but a flimsy red satin robe. Bathed in sunlight, she appeared like an exquisite angel, the sheer red fabric making her even more alluring. Then I noticed the way she held herself, so confident and self-assured.

I shut my mouth and strolled across the living room to the balcony doors. When I started to speak only a strangled croak came out at first. Maria must have heard my footsteps because she turned, smiled and in that perfectly pitched voice greeted me.

"Good morning."

"Morning." I mumbled, struggling to keep my eyes somewhere over her shoulder. "Um, so what do you need me to do?"

"We're going to move a few pieces of furniture around first, and then I have a list of things to be done. I don't drink coffee, but I have some for guests. Fix yourself a cup in the kitchen while I finish getting dressed." Maria crossed the balcony, and I stood aside to let her pass. As she did, I inhaled, relishing her subtle scent. I'd lay money on it being a mixture of lavender and something citrusy, like bergamot. Maria's hair was still damp, and I wondered if it was the shampoo she used, or did she naturally smell like the sexiest woman alive all on her own?

I wandered into the large modern kitchen and noticed she must have done some unpacking last night. A new black coffee maker sat on the marble countertop. I searched the cabinets for coffee, then remembered that since she didn't drink it herself, she probably kept it in the freezer to keep it fresh.

"Bingo." I pulled out a bag of beans and began to make a desperately needed cup of joe. While the coffee brewed, I noticed a sheet of paper on the counter. I glanced down and saw my name scrawled across the top. It was my to-do list, I assumed, and what a quirky list it was.

Caroline,

Please order the following items online. Oh, except for the car, lol. You might have to make a trip to a health food store for the honey and ice cream. Thanks! Maria.

-Premium Organic Matcha Tea from Pangea Organics and licorice root tea

-Zinc and vitamin C lozenges

-9 humidifiers. The old fashioned kind, not the cool mist.

-2 first-aid kits

-Facial steamer

-Dairy-free cashew ice cream and vegan cheddar cheese, the melty kind

The list seemed endless and filled with stuff I'd never heard of before in my life. And vegan cheese? Yuck. It ended with her asking me to locate a 2012 cherry red convertible Mercedes for sale, and Maria wondered where a good karaoke bar was.

"Good, you found the list."

The sheet of paper flew out of my hand. I turned toward her as Maria strolled into the kitchen, then mumbled, "Sorry, you startled me," and bent down to pick it up. While I was bent over, I noticed she had on a pair of black Prada loafers that I used to salivate over when I worked at Montaldo's. As I rose, my eyes stayed glued to her, taking in the casual yet chic clothes. She wore fitted jeans, and a loose blouse made of simple beige cotton with tiny white buttons up the front. She was incredibly sexy, and I wondered if she'd changed her mind about moving furniture and unpacking boxes.

"Yeah, um, some of this stuff I will have to..." I began, but Maria interrupted.

"It doesn't all have to be done at once, just over the next few days. Though, if you could get the raw honey with the comb and the ice cream today I'd be grateful."

I must have made a face because she laughed.

"What? You don't like my taste in food?" She leaned back against the counter, and her cleavage thrust forward. I forced myself to look at the floor.

"No, I um, well, I've never understood why people eat vegan ice cream. Like, why not just eat the real thing?" I asked, then focused my eyes on her right ear so I wouldn't get distracted by her gleaming, perfect teeth.

"Dairy products are bad for the throat. So is coffee." She waggled her eyebrows, then grabbed a thermos out of a cabinet and handed it to me. "Would you fill this with warm water, please? I have to make a quick call and then we can get started."

She left the kitchen, and I fumbled with the faucet to get the water to the right temperature. As I did my imagination went into overdrive, wondering if she'd slept in the nude or...

"Fuck!" Scalding hot water overflowed the thermos. "Be a fucking professional!" I hissed, then prayed she hadn't heard me.

———

We ended up moving a desk from one of the bedrooms into the library and a heavy armoire into the large dressing room adjacent to her bedroom. Somehow Maria did all of this without breaking a sweat or tearing her clothes. I, of course, was a sweaty mess by the time we were done. Then while Maria made more phone calls, I spent another hour hanging and arranging her many clothes. I managed to keep my eyes to myself, and due to lack of sleep and the physical labor was even able to keep my filthy mind under control

Then I found her underwear. More specifically, a pair of skimpy black lace panties. Even more specifically, I might have pressed them against my nose and inhaled like it was the last ounce of oxygen on earth. But instead of stealing them like I really wanted to do, I did the mature thing and set them on top of the armoire. Oh, and that lavender citrus smell that turned me on was *everywhere*. Maria had quite the collection of sexy bras and panties, but she also had a box of what appeared to be comfortable cotton boyshorts that I typically wore.

Now I was at my desk in the seventh floor broom closet of an office, ordering items from Maria's list and brainstorming tweets for her new Twitter account. Maria was in a rehearsal room somewhere, singing her heart out while faking that she couldn't speak to *her* boss Bella. She warned me to keep her secret on the car ride to the rehearsal, and while I wanted to know why she kept up the ruse, I didn't question her about it.

"Knock knock."

I glanced up from my laptop to see the assistant conductor, Peter. "Hey, come on in. Oh, well, there's not a lot of room…" I mumbled, noticing Peter's eyes widen at the thought of being in the tiny space. I'd never been claustrophobic before now, but the broom closet/office was stifling.

"I'm here to drag you to Rehearsal Room D. You've been ordered to take pictures of Maria rehearsing to post on social media, oh, and she wants more warm water." Peter took off his glasses and wiped them on his sleeve. So, I grabbed my phone and off we went, making a brief pit stop in the break room for water.

Rehearsal Room D was small, with a black grand piano in the center plus a few music stands and chairs. Bella was seated behind the piano scribbling something on a sheet of music while Maria stood behind a music stand humming. She gave me a little wave when I walked in and winked. I handed her the water and she nodded her thanks, sipped it, and then took out her pad and pen and scribbled a note.

No pictures of me in profile if at all possible. Only from the front. Oh, and you will need to use lots of filters

Maria had to be kidding me. I glanced up to see if she was serious, but Bella had begun playing the piano. I pulled the phone out of my pocket and fumbled with it until I found the camera function, then almost dropped it when Maria began to sing.

Damn.

I'm not a musician, so I didn't have the words to describe the sounds coming from Maria's throat, but it was like nothing I'd ever heard before. And loud, like really loud. Like this woman would never need a microphone, ever. What amazed me was the transformation her perfect features underwent. Though I couldn't understand a word she sang, which I thought was Italian, I knew she was singing of love. Perfect notes dripped from her mouth, and she made it sound so simple, like anyone could sing like this. Then my eye caught hers and she noticeably faltered, then resumed singing. Bella stopped playing and turned to me.

"Aren't you supposed to be taking pictures?"

It took me a second to register what she'd just asked, then I found my voice. "Oh, sorry, I just... wow. I've heard no one sing like that before in my life. It was breathtaking." I breathed, feeling a flush race up my neck.

"And that's exactly what we want our audiences to feel, too." Bella smiled. "Maria, we'll start again from the beginning. Are you ready to take some pictures, Caroline?" Bella asked. I nodded, then glanced over to see Maria's cheeks were tinged with a subtle pink that hadn't been there before. She avoided my gaze, and I wondered if I'd embarrassed her with my gushing praise.

"Passion, Maria. Sing this aria like you are singing to the love of your life." Bella added. Then he fingers hit the first few chords, and for a split second I wished Maria was singing to me.

CHAPTER
Nine

CAROLINE

KEEPING my cool around Maria became easier over the next two weeks. I was able to be around her nearly every waking minute of the day by enacting the opposite tactic of what I'd tried originally. Instead of denying myself, I embraced my filthy fantasies. Though it came at a cost. I was going through batteries at breakneck speed, and my other toys were being put to use, too.

If I hadn't given in to my urges, I would have been a walking, talking horny mess, and that would've given away my game. I soon realized that getting myself off before work did wonders for my libido and kept me from sniffing her panties when I was alone in her penthouse.

Knowing that I could go home and imagine making love to Maria every night calmed me down. Yes, Maria was the hottest woman I'd ever been around before, but keeping my job was important. The amount of time I spent masturbating to fantasies of my boss allowed me to behave somewhat rationally around her. It cooled the fever, temporarily, at least.

"We trust you. You're a pro. Just don't make her look like a drag queen." The stage director, Peter Gibb, handed me a face chart. "Honestly, this worked out well. You know, you becoming Maria's PA. Instead of sending my new makeup artist Charlie on the road for this solo show, he can stay here and work on the designs for the next opera."

"I'll do my best." I muttered, still a little peeved about not getting the makeup designer job. Peter was being friendly and diplomatic, so I mustered up a smile. "I'll write down Maria's colors so you guys have it for future reference." I placed the face chart on a clipboard.

"Thanks, Caroline." Peter grinned, then left the dressing room.

It was a dress rehearsal for the solo showcase, and I was grateful we were starting off with something so simple. All it involved was a basic stage makeup, and no costume changes. My job was to put on Maria's face and make sure her gown was cleaned and pressed before the show. Oh, and take care of her every whim or desire. I thought I might grow weary of the many details of running Maria's life, but she was so easygoing (and easy on the eyes) that it wasn't difficult.

Bella Lombardi was a much bigger pain in the ass. She was always friendly, funny even, but she was also a demanding perfectionist who on more than one occasion pissed off Maria. But, Bella was also hyper-aware of who her star singer was and did her best to sugarcoat her requests. If she even heard one off-note, she'd insist on Maria singing it again and again, to the point that once Maria had put her foot down and refused to sing anymore that day. Though Maria hadn't told me why she only communicated with notes at work, I suspected it was because of Bella. They'd gone to school together, and Maria needed the detachment of written notes to keep her sane around the conductor.

The door to the dressing room opened. Maria stood there looking like she'd walked off the pages of Vogue magazine. Adorned in a breathtaking silver beaded gown, she exuded an aura of elegance and allure. The gown, meticulously crafted with intricate beading, shimmered with every movement, catching the light and casting a mesmerizing glow.

Maria cleared her throat and nodded toward the director's chair in front of the mirror. I dragged my eyes up her frame and concentrated my focus on her ear. Staring into her glittering dark eyes was dangerous.

"Yes, I'm ready for you." I managed, then turned my back to her both to get my brushes ready and to give myself a moment to collect myself. This wouldn't be easy, because for the very first time I would touch Maria in a professional capacity and I didn't want to lose control. I heard the lock on the dressing room door click, and then Maria settled into the chair behind me. Somehow I had to pretend that she was any other woman getting her makeup done. I breathed in, inhaling her fragrance, then Maria cleared her throat and quietly spoke.

"I'm sick of writing notes, so um, that's why I locked the door. I didn't want anyone to barge in. You know, in case you were wondering."

Glancing up, our eyes locked in the mirror and she lifted a perfect brow. My heartbeat started ramping up, so I resumed fiddling with my brushes as a distraction. Then I picked up the clipboard and realized I didn't have a pen to write Maria's colors on the face chart. I turned around, focusing my gaze over her shoulder.

"Do you have a pen I can borrow?"

Maria pulled it out of the small black purse she always kept by her side. When I took it our fingers brushed, sending little shocks up my spine. "Thanks." I mumbled, then took a deep breath, trying to calm myself.

Pull yourself together, Caroline.

"Are you nervous?" Maria asked, and when I looked at her reflection in the mirror I noted a look of concern.

"Well, yes, a little. It's..." I started, then chuckled. I needed to treat this woman like any other client who'd ever sat down in front of me waiting for their makeup to be applied. "I want you to look your best, and this is our first time working together like this. So, let's figure out the shade of your foundation first." I draped a towel around her neck and began to work.

To say it was torture was an understatement. The feel of her skin under my fingertips was so smooth and soft. I'd had the forethought to wear an apron, on the pretense of keeping my clothes clean, but in reality I knew how my body would react while touching her. My nipples felt like rocks, and smelling that erotic lavender scent seeping out of every cell of her skin and hair made it worse.

C'mon, focus Caroline! Repeat over and over; I do not want Maria Wagner. She's only a fantasy, and she's not good for my career, though the idea of this insanely beautiful woman pushing me up against the dressing room wall and...

"Are you okay?" Maria eyed me, and blood raced up my neck.

"Yeah, of course." I swallowed, turning away for a moment.

When I finished, I stepped back so she could see her reflection in the mirror. Maria's lips twisted into a smile. "Perfect. Looks like me, only magnified. Some artists get so damned heavy-handed. Hate that." She yanked the towel off from around her neck and stood. Then she peered into the mirror once more. "Oh, you got a little something on the shoulder."

She murmured, pointing to a small spot of beige pancake makeup.

"Oops, I'm sorry." I muttered. "I have a…"

"Don't worry about it. Next time we'll do it without my gown on." Maria patted my shoulder, then crossed the room and checked herself out in the mirror from a distance. After adjusting her hair she turned to leave. When she was halfway out the door, Maria asked, "Are you going to watch the rehearsal?"

"Oh, yes, of course. Let me clean up in here first and I'll be right out."

When Maria shut the door, I collapsed into the director's chair and put my face in my hands.

"Oh God." I groaned, wondering how I would be able to do this night after night. Then, I remembered that the next time I applied her makeup, she wouldn't be wearing the gown. I crossed my arms over my chest muttering, "Ouch."

My nipples were so hard it hurt.

———

After rehearsal was over, Maria and I shared an Uber ride back to our neighborhood. Maria was a bundle of nerves over her performance, but I detected a certain degree of hope in her voice.

"It's Friday. We'll be working Tuesday through Sunday next week. Take the next three days off. I doubt I'll need you for anything, but since you live two blocks away…" Maria's voice trailed off as the car pulled up outside of my shabby little apartment building. She'd never seen it before and probably wondered if I'd always lived like an impoverished art student. When I reached for the door handle, she placed her delicate hand on my arm and I jumped in my seat. Then I turned toward hdr, and her eyes twinkled. "Skittish, aren't you?"

My cheeks burned. If Maria only knew that the next three days would be pure hell without seeing her in the flesh. That her hand on my arm burned my skin.

"Anyhow, I just wanted to say thanks." She murmured, and I noticed her hand hadn't moved.

"For what?"

"You know, all the work you've done for me. I've never had an assistant before and you've made my life, I don't know, better somehow. Not just because... I'm babbling, sorry." Maria's cheeks flushed, then she cleared her throat. "All right then. Enjoy your weekend off, and I'll see you Tuesday morning."

The car took off as soon as the door shut. I stood on the street staring after it, then realized Maria might notice, so I hustled to the front door of the building and let myself in. Once inside my apartment, I collapsed on my shabby couch, closed my eyes, and remembered the feel of her skin under my fingers, and the touch of her hand on my arm.

Maria's final words in the car played on a loop in my mind, the way she'd thanked me, and the blush of embarrassment that colored her cheeks as she spoke.

"Stop it." I muttered, then stood to go into the kitchen. Halfway there I turned back toward the couch, knowing there wasn't a chance in hell I'd be able to eat. I grabbed the remote and was going to mindlessly watch cooking shows, but tossed it back on the cluttered coffee table. I kicked my shoes off, curled up on the couch, and screamed wordlessly into a throw pillow, hoping my neighbors wouldn't hear.

CHAPTER
Ten

CAROLINE

I WOKE up face down on the couch, my phone buzzing on the coffee table in front of me. I turned over and yawned, the last wisps of a dream I couldn't recall evaporating away. Someone had sent me a text, and my heart skipped a beat when I realized it might be Maria. When I saw who the message was from, I nearly flung the phone across the room.

My ex-girlfriend, Marilyn.

Since it was a little after nine Saturday morning, I was reasonably sure she wasn't drunk texting. We'd broken up three years ago, and about every six months she'd call or text while bombed out of her mind. It was always the same thing. She missed me, wished things had gone differently, and would I be interested in hanging out sometime soon?

The first few times I went along with it, swept up in a tide of nostalgia. Gone were the bad times, the drunken arguments and the constant feeling of unease. Then, after *hanging out,* Marilyn would show her true colors. She knew every insecurity of mine and played them like an out of tune piano, jangly notes that made me cringe.

"Hell no. I'm not replying to that." I grumbled and laid the phone down on the table. It buzzed again. "Marilyn, you're working my last good gay nerve." I stood, walked into the bathroom, and took a long hard look at myself in the mirror. Finally, for the first time in three years, I was truly over her. The angst and despair I used to feel whenever she'd text or call was absent, replaced by irritation and a sad sense of loss.

"I loved you once, Marilyn, I really did. But, it's time for you to move on. I have." I murmured, then walked back into the living room to see what Marilyn wanted. There were three texts. The first two were from my ex, while the third one was from Maria.

> Sorry
>
> I know it's your day off, but I need a few things and don't know where to find them
>
> Rooibos Tea
>
> Cough Syrup
>
> Vicks VapoRub
>
> Sugar Free Vitamin C lozenges
>
> If you could get them for me I'll make it up to you soon
>
> I swear I'll leave you alone for the rest of the weekend

That didn't sound good. I texted Maria back.

Are U sick?

A minute passed, and I wondered if she'd changed her mind. Finally, she replied.

Yes

I tossed the phone on to the couch, ran into the bathroom and turned on the hot water in the shower. It was an old building, and the water took a couple of minutes to warm up. Then I raced into the living room and sent her a text back.

Jumping into the shower now

Be there asap

———

An hour and a half later I showed up at Maria's apartment with bags of medicines, teas and my secret cold and flu medicine; Mom's chicken soup.

After two weeks of working for her, we'd grown comfortable enough for me to just let myself in. When I opened her door, it was like walking into a hot humid jungle, minus the plants and creepy critters. By now, all nine of the humidifiers I'd ordered for Maria had arrived, and she must have had each one running at full blast. I put the bags down in the kitchen, found a stock pot and began warming up the chicken soup I'd had frozen in my freezer.

"What are you doing?"

Maria was standing in the kitchen doorway wearing her customary skin-hugging t-shirt and pink sweatpants. Her tan arms glistened in the humid air. I forced my eyes up to face level and replied, "I have a secret weapon against colds, flus, and any other pesky crap you can think of. My mom's chicken soup."

"You don't have to do all this. I gave you the weekend off and..."

I held my hand up. "Stop. It's no problem at all. Oh, and I got you the stuff you wanted." I detected a hint of congestion in her voice, and Maria's eyes were bloodshot. "What the hell is rooibos tea, anyway?"

Maria grinned, and I noticed the darkness under her eyes. She looked like she hadn't slept. "It's an herbal tea from South Africa, also known as red bush tea. Rooibos is loaded with antioxidants and other stuff my voice teacher claimed would cure anything."

"I'll heat up some water for you." I reached into the cabinet next to the stove and pulled out the kettle.

"So, does your mother live close by? How did she make this soup so fast?" Maria asked, yawning at the same time. I glanced up to see her stretching her arms over her head, pulling the too-tight t-shirt up and exposing her flat stomach.

"I made it from her recipe. Mom lives in Youngstown, Ohio." I turned on the burner, then opened the box of tea. "When I was a kid, she'd make this whenever we were sick, and I swear by it. Didn't your mom have a special thing she'd do for you when you were ill?"

"The same as your mother. *Sopa de Pollo* and Vicks VapoRub were her remedies." Maria replied, surprising me.

"I thought you were German, or Swiss?" I asked. Marilyn was Mexican-American, and I recognized the Spanish name of chicken soup.

"I am. My mother is from Puerto Rico, and my father was from Berlin. He died when I was young, so Mom moved to Connecticut where her family had relocated. She's an amazing cook, but we're not very..." Maria said. But then the kettle whistled. She crossed the room before I could react, reached around me and grabbed it off the burner. Her lavender scent permeated the air, and it took considerable self-control not to grab her t-shirt and inhale it from the source. Instead, I decided to get the object of my lust into another room so I could focus on the food.

"Go watch TV or something. I'll take care of your lunch."

"Seriously, Caroline, you don't have to..." Maria started, but I cut her off.

"I have no other plans, plus you have a big week coming up. If you're not healthy, that means I'm not working. So let me do my job, which is making sure you are happy, healthy and ready to perform." What I didn't add was that if I wasn't here, I'd be sitting at home thinking about her, with the help of my vibrator and porn.

"You're the boss." Maria grinned, throwing her hands up in the air in mock surrender. She placed a teabag in her mug of water and left the kitchen.

———

"Here you go." I placed a tray on the coffee table in front of her with *two* bowls of soup. If I was going to be here cooking for Maria, she'd have to put up with me eating with her. We didn't spend much time doing non-work related things. Our days were filled with rehearsals, social media, and me running errands. Aside from the fact that she was a somewhat famous singer who was neurotic about her voice, I knew very little about what made Maria tick.

"This is amazing." Maria murmured after the first spoonful. "Thank you."

I started in on my bowl, occasionally sneaking glances at Maria. She had a blanket covering her lap, holding the warm bowl in one hand and the spoon in another. With each spoonful, she seemed to appreciate the flavors, allowing the comforting warmth to envelop her senses. Of course that was my imagination. Who knows how she really felt about the damned soup, but my brain went into overdrive whenever I was around Maria.

"So, what do you do for fun?" I asked after she'd finished her bowl. Maria turned away from me, snatched a tissue out of a box next to her, and wiped her nose. Even with a cold, she was still stunning. "Besides turning your apartment into the biggest sauna in Raleigh."

Maria rolled her eyes and laughed, which turned into a tiny cough. "Well, the reason for the sauna is that I can't afford to get sick, and the heat and humidity is best for my throat. That's why I'm always drinking warm water."

"I figured that about the water. So, aside from singing, what do you like to do?" I hoped I wasn't overstepping a boundary, but I wanted to know what made Maria tick. You know, so I could either find a reason not to be attracted, or so I could add another layer to my hopeless fantasy about her.

Maria paused, staring straight ahead at the blank television screen on the opposite wall. "Well, I read mostly. Sometimes I play online backgammon. But, my career is my thing. I don't have a lot of time for much else."

For a split second, I felt pity. Here she was, one of the most beautiful women I'd ever seen, who had a career most people would envy, and she literally had no life outside of her work.

"You need to go out more, because it sounds like you live in a retirement village or something." *Shit.* That didn't come out right. "I'm sorry. I shouldn't have said that." I mumbled, my cheeks burning. In the blurry reflection on the flat screen TV I noticed Maria's shoulders stiffen, and then she sighed.

"I've spent many years working, and as you are learning, it isn't an easy job. When I lost my voice…" Maria's tone grew somber, "I thought I'd lost everything. Singing is everything to me, and if that means not having much of a life?" She shrugged then pulled another tissue out of the box.

"Hey, do you remember that list you gave me on my first day?" I asked. Maria nodded. "At the very bottom you asked me where a good karaoke bar was. As soon as you're better, I'm taking you to Flex. Every Sunday night they have *scaryoke*, which is filled with non-singers like me singing off key. It's fun." As soon as the words popped out of my mouth, I regretted it. Flex was a gay bar, mostly for men, and I was still clueless about which team Maria played on.

Maria laughed. "I love karaoke. It's fun to sing stuff non-opera related. Maybe after the performances are done next week, we can go." Then she grabbed the remote and switched on the television. "This is the first time I've turned it on since I moved in. I usually watch documentaries, but I bet that's not your thing. Am I right?"

I swiveled my head to answer, and she was lightly biting down on her lower lip. I nodded, though I would've watched anything Maria wanted just so I could sit next to her for a while longer.

"What do you want to watch?" Maria navigated to the guide channel, and I felt her shoulder press against mine.

Well, I guessed that meant she wanted me to hang out. My heart thumped in my chest. "When I'm feeling crappy, I watch eighties movies. I don't know why, but they always make me feel better."

"Okay." Maria said as the TV listings ran down the screen. Then I saw the one movie I *didn't* want to see. The film that virtually guaranteed that my inappropriate fantasies about my boss would become even more pathetic and desperate.

"Oh, that's a good one, and it's from the eighties too." Maria clicked the remote. And of course, it was *that* movie, the one that always made me cry. I snuck a glance at her and noticed Maria's broad smile. She really wanted to watch it.

"*Fuck.*" I muttered under my breath, then hoped she hadn't heard.

"Excuse me?" Maria lifted an eyebrow. "Did you want to watch something else?"

"No no, I love *Moonstruck*. It's one of my favorite films of all time."

———

"That movie gets to you, huh?" Maria asked, looking down at the crumpled kleenex in my hand. I nodded, and she switched off the TV. "Me too."

I couldn't tell if she'd cried or not since her eyes were already red from her cold. A cold I might catch since I'd been breathing in her air for the last two hours while her shoulder stayed glued to mine. But I didn't care. Maria could have had Ebola and I still would've watched Cher and Nicolas Cage fall in love onscreen by her side. We sat there for a few more moments until the silence and tension-filled air became too much for me to bear. I rose to my feet.

"Let me head on out. There's more soup on the stove in case you're hungry. Do you need anything else?" I asked, hoping she'd ask me to stay, but afraid that she would, too.

Maria shook her head no, then stood up and walked me to the door.

"Thanks." Maria murmured. "I'm glad you were here with me. I get a little… too much in my own head sometimes." Her voice caught at the end of her sentence, and when I met Maria's gaze, there was a heat I'd never seen before, though it was probably because she was sick. She opened the door and stood back to let me walk by.

"Anytime." I murmured. "See you Tuesday."

I stood in front of the elevator and pressed the down button, then spun around. "You know, if you…" I began, but the door was already shut.

CHAPTER
Eleven

MARIA

"I WISH I could change into my gown here instead of at the theater. Hell, I'd rather perform in my sweats." I grumbled. Elise laughed. I'd called my former vocal teacher in Italy, hoping she would calm me down. Tonight was my first public performance since the debacle at the Royal Opera in London, and I kept reliving the horror of that night, an endless loop playing in the back of my head.

"Maria, trust your voice. It is better than it has ever been, unless you've allowed that conductor to..."

"Elise, no, Bella has been a pleasure to work with, though I've had to say no to over-singing a few times. If she had her way we'd be rehearsing around the clock." I rubbed the back of my neck and sighed. "I figured out that keeping communication to written notes works best with Bella, that way I don't tax my vocal cords and..."

"Why?" She interrupted. "There's nothing wrong with your voice, unless there is something you aren't telling me. Oh, I need to put the phone down for a sec." I heard her fumble with something, then she began again. "Sorry, I need a glass of wine for this."

"Wish I could join you for one." I muttered. Alcohol wasn't a singer's best friend, but I used to enjoy the occasional glass of wine, until my voice abandoned me.

"Obviously you are going on stage in a couple of hours, so wine would be a bad idea. But, after the show, a glass or two wouldn't hurt... Maria, I know you're scared, but it will be okay. It will be more than okay, because once you experience performing in front of an audience again and realize your voice will hold up by singing the way I taught you..."

"Elina, but what happens if..."

"Maria. Take a deep breath and calm down." Elise commanded.

I'd been pacing the length of my balcony, so I walked inside and sat on the sofa, placing a hand on my thigh to keep my leg from bouncing.

"Have you eaten anything?" She knew me well.

I hated eating when I was nervous. My stomach churned all weekend, well, except for when Caroline had been around. I wondered if I could keep a bowl of that delicious soup down? No. It wasn't worth risking it.

"I can't eat right now." I mumbled, then glanced at the clock on the wall. I needed to head to the theater soon. "Look, thanks for listening to me, but you're right. I just have to get this over with. I trust you, and if you think I'm ready, then I am."

"*Toi toi toi*, my dear friend. You will be a star all over again, I just know it. Call or text me after the performance." Elise disconnected the call before I had a chance to say goodbye, probably tired of dealing with my neurotic fear of failure. I laid my head back on the cushion and shut my eyes for a moment, willing myself to be strong.

"You've got this. Plus, Caroline will be there, and you must do well for her. If I fail, then there will be two of us out of a job." I said aloud. Then I saw Caroline's face in my head. The woman had the most piercing eyes I'd ever seen. Caroline eyes, gray with a hint of blue, sparkled when she laughed, which wasn't often enough. If I thought I was a bundle of nerves, Caroline was even worse. She was prone to dropping things, and her long, slim fingers were always trembling. Her nervousness only fed into my own, but Caroline *was* superb at her job. It had been easy to work with her, but for the first couple of weeks it had felt awkward being around her so much. Well, until we watched that movie together. It was the first time we'd connected in a non-professional way and it felt good, like we could actually be friends. I'd never had too many of those. The opera world was too cutthroat for that. Maybe it was because she wasn't a singer or musician that I felt comfortable around Caroline?

"Ha!" I laughed, then opened my eyes and glanced out the balcony doors at the fading sunlight. "It's not because I feel safe, or because I want a friend. Caroline is a good-looking woman, and it's been a very long time since I..."

The phone buzzed next to me. "Speak of the devil." It was Caroline, telling me a car would be downstairs in five minutes.

"Toi toi toi." I whispered, then grabbed my phone and keys and hurried off to discover whether I would be forever doomed as a failed singer or if I still had a chance to be a star.

———

"Everything's ready. All you have to do is perform." Caroline handed me a thermos of warm water. My gown was perfectly pressed and Caroline's makeup brushes were spread across the counter. She flicked on the lights surrounding the mirror and gestured for me to be seated, but stopped me. "Let's do your makeup before you get changed. I don't want to ruin your gown."

"Yeah, that's right. We already discussed that." I murmured, then Caroline took the thermos from me and I walked over to the metal clothes rack on the other side of the dressing room. I unbuttoned my blouse, hung it up, then froze for a moment. Changing clothes backstage was nothing new for me. I'd done it hundreds of times in front of rooms filled with other performers. Glancing over at Caroline, I noticed she had her back turned, and was fiddling with her makeup brushes. Then my eyes ventured further south, resting on her firm round ass. "Damn." I muttered, then turned my attention back to the clothes rack. My stomach fluttered, and I knew if I had to take my clothes off in front of Caroline, I might cross a boundary a boss should never cross with an employee. It was one thing for me to think Caroline was attractive, but to show her? That was totally out of bounds.

"Did you say something?" Caroline asked, still messing with her brushes.

"No, sorry, just clearing my throat." I muttered. Irrationally, I snuck a glance toward Caroline to make sure she was still turned away from me. She was, so I kicked off my loafers and was about to unbutton my slacks when Caroline's phone rang.

"Caroline Frank." She answered, then leaned against the counter facing me. I noticed a slight flush to her cheeks, and as usual she avoided my gaze. My fingers were still fumbling with the top button of my pants, so I turned away.

"I'll be right there." Caroline said, then disconnected the call. "Bella wants me. Be right back."

As soon as the door shut behind her I changed out of my slacks and stepped into the gown, almost as fast as if I was doing a costume change for the stage.

"I'll just leave it unzipped, and Caroline can drape a towel around my shoulders." I felt silly, stupid even. Then I sat down in front of the mirror and laughed. "What is wrong with me? I've been completely nude in front of tons of performers without giving it a second thought. Caroline is a professional, and I doubt she's giving me a second thought." As soon as I whispered the last sentence aloud, I wondered if that was true. When we watched *Moonstruck* together, she'd been glued to my side. None of my other female friends had ever been that cozy with me, unless they wanted something more.

"No, I'd be able to tell if Caroline was…"

The door to the dressing room opened, and Caroline walked in, shaking her head. "Sorry about that. Bella wanted to know if you were doing okay or not. I told her you were feeling great, just a mild case of nerves which was perfectly normal."

"It's her job to know these things. Bella is an excellent conductor. Glad you lied for me, because I feel like I'm going to be sick." I said. Caroline wrapped a towel around my neck, clipped it into place, then rubbed my shoulder.

"I didn't lie. You do have a case of the nerves, but I've heard you sing and know that once you are on that stage everything will be awesome." Caroline replied, then picked up the pancake makeup and started brushing it on my face.

Caroline's belief in me was reassuring, but I was still terrified. Without thinking, I reached for her, holding her wrist still. "When my voice abandoned me on stage in front of thousands of people, I thought my life was over. Thank you, Caroline, for believing in me more than I believe in myself."

The brush fell out of Caroline's hand, clattering to the floor. Our eyes met, and for the first time since I'd signed the contract with the North Carolina Opera, I felt calm, serene almost. I let go of her wrist and she bent down and picked up the brush. Caroline fumbled through her brushes, pulled out a new one and went back to work, though I could feel her hand trembling against my skin.

Something passed between us, an understanding of sorts, a sudden depth of trust which I'd rarely experienced with anyone.

"Look up to the ceiling." Caroline murmured, and then her hand was against my cheek as she drew the eyeliner underneath my upper lashes, her other hand on my shoulder holding me still. When she was done with one eye, she switched hands to do the other, and the feel of her fingers on my shoulder made me shudder. A subtle warmth spread through my limbs, and suddenly I wanted, no, *needed* to know everything about this woman. It had been years since I felt this way. When I lost my voice my sole focus was on getting it back. Now I felt like a teenager again, navigating emotional waters I'd long forgotten about.

"Close your eyes, Maria." Caroline commanded. A moment later, the stroke of her brush drew black liquid above my lashes. I felt the warmth of her breath against my cheek, and for a moment I forgot to breathe. When she was done with both eyes, I gasped for air, then laughed nervously. Caroline's touch was entirely appropriate. It was what she was paid to do. My response to it was unbidden, and wrong.

"Almost done." Caroline said, then she dropped another brush, bent over to pick it up, and the sight of her ass for just that split second made my mouth turn bone dry. My body stiffened, and I felt heat in between my legs.

"Sorry about that. I'm all thumbs today." Caroline muttered. My nipples were so hard, and I hoped she wouldn't notice when it came time to zip up the gown. "Let me put this lip balm on you." She mumbled, and then her index finger pressed against my lips, slowly rubbing back and forth.

I groaned and felt blood racing to my cheeks. Caroline's

finger froze for a moment, then she turned back to her supplies. I glanced into the mirror to see her face, and Caroline's eyes were closed. When she opened them, she fumbled with her cosmetics. I glanced away before she caught me staring.

"Now I'm going to put a stain on your lips. It's very natural looking, and it won't come off during your performance." Caroline placed a drop of a brownish-pink liquid on her finger and once again she pressed it against my lips, rubbing the color in. I wanted to open my mouth, take that finger inside me, imagine what her skin tasted like if we ever…

The door to the dressing room flew open and Caroline jerked back, her hip hitting the counter. It was Bella.

"I'm about to take the stage. You're on in five minutes."

CHAPTER

Twelve

CAROLINE

"I'M glad you found this car for me to lease. I'm tempted to buy one of my own." Maria smoothed her hand over the top of the dash, then switched on the radio. "Could you find National Public Radio?"

We were in a cherry-red convertible Mercedes, and it was magnificent. The cream-colored seats were covered in the smoothest leather, and it had to be the ritziest car I'd ever been in. The only bad thing was the rain, since we couldn't put the top down. I fiddled with the radio until I found the public radio station, then sank back into the luxurious seat.

The performances in Raleigh and Greensboro had been massive hits. Every show sold out, and the reviews were excellent. As a result of this, Maria perked up, and her moods leveled out. She'd even begun speaking to Bella and the rest of the staff, dispensing with the notes altogether.

But on opening night, I'd felt insane tension brewing between us. I couldn't tell if it was my imagination or not, but I'd swear Maria was attracted to me. Whenever I touched her, she'd blush, and her breathing would become staggered. This continued with every show since then. Whenever I had to apply Maria's makeup, I had this bizarre combination of lust and dread, because she was totally off limits. Maria was my boss, and I wasn't about to lose my job because I couldn't keep my hands to myself.

So, I did what I had to do, though maintaining my composure was tricky. I'd prepare mentally by looking at unattractive pictures on my phone before Maria sat in the makeup chair. Stuff like car wrecks, politicians and ax murderers. This only worked for the first minute or so, because as soon as my fingers grazed her smooth skin, I'd become flustered. But no matter what, I behaved like a professional. And to her credit, so did Maria. I even noticed that whenever she had to change clothes she'd send me on an errand.

Damn it.

We were heading to Charlotte for the final two shows at the Belk Theater. It had been a crazy week, and I was looking forward to it being over with. Maria and I would be staying in a hotel near the theater, along with Bella and the musicians. Of course, Bella and Maria got the best rooms with all the perks, while the musicians and I were stuck with the cheapest ones.

Our schedule was tight. As soon as we arrived, we were going straight to the local public radio station for an interview. Then, Maria was doing another interview with the music critic from the newspaper at the hotel. While she was in the second interview, I'd be unpacking her bags, setting up a humidifier in her room, and resisting the urge to climb under the blankets of her bed and indulge in frantic masturbation. Which would be a pain in the ass since I'd have to remake the bed, but then I could pretend that we had..?

Pathetic.

Afterward, Maria would meet with Bella to go over the upcoming performance. Then, we would get a few minutes to shower and change before she did a meet and greet with fans who'd spent extra to shake her hand before the show. The world of classical music was very similar to pop, except not as well publicized. Maria was being heralded as the comeback kid, the singer who defied the odds and got her voice back. If tonight and tomorrow's performances went well, she'd probably be right back on top, with the media coverage to prove it.

"I'm glad you're here with me."

My head snapped in Maria's direction, wondering if I'd heard her correctly. I turned down the radio. "Sorry, I um, couldn't hear you."

"You being here is, well, helping me stay strong. I didn't think I'd ever be in this position again. My best-case scenario two years ago when I lost my voice was to teach music, or find a career in another field. I'm scared." Maria whispered the last two words. She took her eyes off the road for a split second and met my gaze. "But, you've been the best, Caroline. Like, just knowing you're by my side has kept me sane."

Maria's right hand left the steering wheel for a brief moment, reaching toward my leg. Then it stopped mid-air, and she moved it back to the wheel.

Time slowed down, and I felt something blocking my throat, making it hard to breathe. Finally, I stammered, "Thanks, Maria. Just, you know, doing my job."

———

It wasn't just me feeling this thing, whatever it was between us. We spent the last half of the trip in silence, listening to the radio. I thought I was going to accompany Maria to both interviews, but when we pulled into the parking lot of the hotel, she told me I wasn't needed. Instead, Maria wanted me to unpack her things and go to the auditorium and wait for her there. She didn't even go up to her room, just handed me the room key and bolted from the lobby.

Most personal assistants would be grateful for a few hours to themselves. Instead of fetching countless glasses of warm water and screening her phone calls, I'd actually have a chance to be alone, to chill out doing whatever I wanted. This would probably involve my poor, overworked vibrator, though I'd do that in my own room. However, there was a problem with that plan.

I wanted to be with Maria, and no fantasy I could conjure up in my filthy mind could compare to the real thing.

———

The dressing room at the Belk Theater wasn't much bigger than my dinky office back in Raleigh. Because of the small humidifier I'd brought, the room was steamy. Only half the bulbs around the mirror worked, which didn't matter because it kept fogging up thanks to the humidifier. Maria was such a diva when it came to her throat.

After setting up my supplies, I noticed the time. Maria would be here any minute, so I grabbed the empty thermos out of my bag and was about to go in search for a source of warm water when the door to the dressing room flew open.

"... I gave Roger Baker front row seats, so make sure you focus on him occasionally. Hell, wink and flirt if you think he'll write a great review." Bella said, following Maria into the crowded dressing room. "This is the star dressing room? You would've been better off using the one down the hall meant for the chorus. Oh, Caroline, play up Maria's eyes tonight. We have a critic to charm." Bella clapped me on the shoulder and left.

Maria shrugged off her jacket and kicked off her shoes, which she usually did before sending me from the dressing room so she could change without me ogling her. Maria glanced down at my hand with the thermos and pointed at it.

"Would you mind getting me some water, please?"

When I returned Maria was seated in front of the mirror, a small white towel draped around her creamy shoulders. She'd apparently tried to wipe the steam from the mirror, but it was already steaming up again. I handed the thermos to Maria. She nodded and stared somewhere over my shoulder. I picked up my apron, then tossed it in my bag. Since I'd morosely attended to my base needs only an hour and a half ago, I saw no reason to add another layer of clothing while in this muggy room.

"Would you turn off the humidifier, please?" Maria asked, surprising me. "The room is so small. It's overwhelming. I don't want to be sweating before I even hit the stage."

I resisted the urge to let her know she looked like a Goddess, with a sheen of perspiration glistening on her skin. It was too bad she wasn't performing naked, because the audience would go wild.

After I switched it off, I wiped at the mirror again, then remembered an old trick. I rifled through my supplies until I found what I needed; shaving cream. Then I covered the mirror with it.

"What are you doing?" Maria asked. "And why do you have shaving cream in your makeup case?"

"I have shaving cream just in case you need it. Better to be overprepared than under." I replied, then wiped the shaving cream off the glass. "Voila. Fog free mirror, at least for a day or two."

Maria gazed at her reflection inquisitively, then shrugged her shoulders and nodded. "Whatever works."

Before I applied her makeup, I had to tissue off her face because of the humidity, otherwise the cosmetics would slide off her skin. Maria's eyes were closed, and when I touched her she flinched, and a tiny kernel of self-doubt churned in my gut.

What happened to the woman thanking me in the car for being with her?

"Are you feeling all right?" I murmured, then pressed foundation primer into her skin with my palms. Maria didn't respond, so I pretended like I'd said nothing, and that she hadn't ignored me. I spun around and grabbed the concealer and a brush off the counter and turned back to Maria. This time her eyes were wide open, looking directly into mine.

"Would you, um, look up at the ceiling?" I asked. Maria did as I asked, and I painted the makeup under her eyes and then around the corners of her nose. I set the brush down on the counter and patted the makeup in place with my ring finger.

"Fuck it." Maria muttered, shaking her head back and forth.

"Maria, what's going on?" I leaned back, my palms gripping the edge of the counter. Her eyes met mine, and I felt my cheeks darken as I noticed Maria's eyes were dilated. "Are you okay?"

"No," she grunted, never taking her eyes off of mine. Maria parted her lips, and I felt my knees grow weak. She got to her feet, swaying a fraction of an inch before placing a hand on each of my shoulders. Her hand slid up the curve of my neck and I felt her fingers in the back of my hair.

"Maria, are you…"

The towel around her neck slid to the floor, exposing her black lacy bra. Maria pulled me into her chest, and then her lips pressed into the soft flesh under my ear. My hands gripped her sides to keep from falling, and a deep moan I'd never made before in my life came out of my throat. Maria's fingertips grazed my cheek, and my breath hitched. She stared at me for a long moment, then slowly her face came closer. Time stood still as her lips met mine, then it transformed into an electric kiss, little shocks passing from her mouth to mine. I felt her fingers kneading the back of my neck, and my legs trembled when her tongue dipped inside my mouth. Finally, Maria broke the kiss.

"Caroline, oh Caroline, I've wanted you so much." Maria pulled back, then she combed her fingers through my hair.. "You are driving me…"

There was a knock at the door.

"Five minutes!" A woman's voice yelled, then came the sound of footsteps rushing away.

Maria loosened her hold on me and sighed, then she gently pushed me back.

"I'm sorry." She murmured. "I shouldn't have done that."

"No, don't be sorry, because… sit. Let me at least get some mascara and powder on you." I looked up into her eyes that were glistening down into mine. Maria's lips parted as if to speak, then she shut them and did what I asked.

Four minutes later Maria was out the door, not another word spoken between us.

CHAPTER
Thirteen

CAROLINE

MARIA'S PERFORMANCE in Charlotte was a colossal success. The next day, the reviews had come in and they were glowing. Maria had been praised for her beautiful voice and captivating performance.

As far as my performance went, it must not have been up to snuff, because ever since that night in the dressing room when we kissed, Maria had kept me at arm's length. She only spoke when she needed something, and half the time she did it via text message. Maria also kept me away from her penthouse, so I spent the majority of my time in my cramped office or running errands around town. Thankfully, I was also heavily involved with pre-production duties. Since I was in charge of Maria's makeup and wardrobe, I met regularly with Peter the stage director and the makeup and wardrobe designers.

Two weeks after that fateful night, we were deep in rehearsals for the first opera of the season, Cosi Fan Tutte, by some german dude named Mozart. I spent hours listening to performances of it on YouTube, hoping it would give me something to talk about with Maria, besides telling her the daily schedule over the phone. These conversations usually went something like this.

"Maria, hi. Just letting you know that your interview with the Raleigh News Observer Style editor has been postponed to the fifth."

"Thank you for letting me know. Is there anything else?" Maria's voice had that detached quality I'd come to dread.

"Um, well, I listened to Cosi last night." I'd said, waiting for her to respond. Nothing. "I can't wait to hear you sing the part of Despina. That aria she sings about…"

"Sorry, Caroline, I'm needed at rehearsal. We'll talk later." And she'd hung up, and I'd moaned with frustration, wondering what the hell was wrong with me. There was a boundary between boss and employee, and while yes, Maria had crossed it, she'd also done the correct thing and backed away. She was never rude, and kept our interactions one hundred percent professional, which was what I wanted.

But that didn't stop me from going home every damn night after work and pulling one of her t-shirts I'd snatched out of her laundry and holding it against my chest. Then, it would inch up to my face where I'd inhale her scent, and for the first time in my life I'd literally swooned. Like, if I were standing up I'd have fallen down, thanks to my wobbling knees and pounding heart. Then, I'd throw the shirt across the room and swear to myself that this had to stop. I was making things much harder for myself, both physically and mentally. Then, while still cursing my lack of control, I'd strip my clothes off, pick up the t-shirt and after a frantic few minutes with my vibrator, I'd be filled with more regret, angst and tears.

Maria was wrong for crossing that boundary, but she'd done the right thing by becoming strictly professional. Now it was on me to adhere to the rules, because I knew the consequences, and I was not about to let the highest paid job of my career go down the toilet. It was either stomp my feelings for my boss into oblivion, or find another useless job schlepping lipstick behind a department store makeup counter.

———

"Has anyone told you what a perfect ass you have, young lady?"

A woman's voice drawled behind me, then I felt a pinch on my left cheek. I spun around to behold Loretta Anne, her bright-pink lips slyly pressed together. She winked, then draped an arm over my shoulder. We were in the hallway in front of Human Resources. I was there for a legitimate work-related reason, while I thought she was in search of mischief.

"Don't take me seriously, Caroline. I love sexy men, though the fairer sex has tempted me a few times." She kissed me on the cheek, then pulled a white handkerchief out of her purse and wiped the remnants of her lipstick off. I laughed for a second, and then it dawned on me that the only person who wanted me was an eccentric southern belle whose hair color changed on a weekly basis. Currently, it was a vivid salmon shade.

"Why so glum?" She asked. "Rehearsals are going well, and Maria Wagner is a dream to work with."

My phone buzzed in my back pocket, saving me from her banter. "This is Caroline."

"I need to speak with you about something important." Bella's sharp voice always intimidated me. "Come to my office. I only have a few minutes."

"Sure, I just need to drop some forms off with Angela and I'll be right there." I turned to Loretta Anne and shrugged my shoulders. "Bella wants to meet me in her office. Why does she always scare the hell out of me?" I leaned back against the wall and sighed.

"Afraid of Bella? Sweetie, she's a big pussycat. But, she's also got a lot of pressure on her to bring in the money. Don't be nervous around her. Bella is good people. If she wasn't, I'd never have allowed her to marry my best friend, Lilith."

"Didn't you tell me they met here? And wasn't Bella Lilith's boss?" A flicker of hope made my heart skip a beat.

"Well, yes. Bella is the big boss around here, which is why she went after Lilith. Bella isn't the type of woman who follows the rules. She's..." Angela's door opened and Loretta patted me on the shoulder and hustled down the hall. Something told me that she and Angela weren't exactly pals.

"Do you have those credit card receipts for Maria's account?" She held her hand out, and I noticed the mauve polish on her index finger was chipped. I handed her the file, and she shut her office door without another word.

"You're welcome." I muttered, then scurried down the hall to Bella's office. When I got there, I noticed the blinds were closed on the floor-to-ceiling glass walls, which was never a good sign. I took a deep breath and knocked, and it immediately opened. I jumped, startled.

"Sorry, Bella. You scared..."

"Come in." She grumbled and gestured toward the leather loveseat in front of her desk. Bella slammed the door shut, then walked behind her desk and sat. She tilted her head to the side and said nothing at first. I felt perspiration dripping down my sides, and a chill ran through me. Then a horrible thought raced through my mind.

Did Bella know about the kiss?

"So, um, what did you want to see me about?" I mumbled, unable to meet her gaze. Bella steepled her fingers under her chin and continued to stare. "If it's about the wardrobe or makeup for the show, I can show you my…"

"Calm down, Caroline." Bella sighed, then leaned back in her chair. "What's wrong with Maria?"

My mouth dropped open, and I wondered what she meant. "Well, I wasn't aware there was any problem with her."

"Maria's been acting strange, even for her." Bella rolled her eyes, stood and began pacing around the office. "There's nothing wrong with her performance. Maria's voice is superb. In fact, it's better than it was when we were in school together. But ever since we did the shows in Northern Virginia she's been…" Bella leaned against the desk in front of me and threw her hands in the air, "…cold and aloof. I mean, even when she was only talking to you and passing us those stupid notes, she was always friendly."

"How did you know Maria was only talking to…"

"I know everything around here. Remember that. Now, let me ask you again. Do you have any clue why my star soprano is giving me and everyone else around here the cold shoulder?" Bella asked, then sat back down on her side of the desk. "Well?"

"I don't know what to say, Bella. Maria is acting the same as she always has." I lied.

"Bullshit." Bella shook her head back and forth a couple of times and grimaced. "Maria's not even hanging out with you anymore. When she first started, you and her were inseparable. Maria had you at every rehearsal, and I could sense a real bond developing between the two of you."

My heart sank, and instantly I thought of us watching movies together on his couch, eating my mom's chicken soup together.

I fucking missed that.

I finally met Bella's inquisitive gaze. Damn it, I hadn't realized how obvious it must have been to everybody we worked with that Maria and I had been growing close. My mouth opened to say something, anything, but the words dried on my tongue.

"Are you sure you don't know what's up with Maria, because I need to know." Bella asked, then I thought of being fired from my last job and realized Bella was the last person on earth I should talk to about this. This woman had the power to fire me, and the odds were stacked against me if she ever found out about the kiss.

"No, no, I really don't know anything. I'll keep my eyes open and if I learn…"

"Let me make this plain to you. I hired you to not only be Maria's PA and makeup artist, but to also make that woman happy. A happy singer is a productive singer. If she's in a foul mood, then everyone else around her is miserable too. Ask me how I know." Bella put her face in her hands and sighed, then looked up at me. "Make Maria happy again. I don't care how you do it, but I need this season to be a tremendous success, and without a happy star, it won't happen."

If Bella only knew how I really wanted to make Maria happy, she'd hand me my walking papers. But then I remembered her and Lilith, and for a brief second I entertained the thought of asking Bella about it. No, that would be foolish. I looked up again and noticed Bella had an eyebrow raised, and I realized I must have muttered something.

"Um, sorry Bella, just thinking aloud about how I can…"

"I need to get back to rehearsals." Bella stalked across the office and flung the door open. When I got there, she put her arm across the doorway, preventing me from leaving. I glanced up into her dark, flat eyes.

"Make Maria happy. Your job depends on it."

CHAPTER
Fourteen

MARIA

"WHAT'S WRONG? You don't sound like yourself," Elise remarked, concerned. I pressed the phone to my chest, taking a deep breath. Even miles away in Italy, I couldn't hide my emotions from her. Putting the phone back to my ear, I responded, "Oh, it's nothing. Everything's going fine."

"Is it about the upcoming opera? Cosi Fan Tutte, right? I assume you're playing Despina, and you know that role inside out," Elise inquired, followed by a pause. "Wait, there's something else, isn't there?"

"No, I'm just nervous about performing on stage in an actual opera. It's much different from a simple recital," I confessed, revealing one of the reasons for my frazzled nerves. She was too far away to help with my more pressing concern.

"When do the performances begin?"

"On June 24. Two weeks from tomorrow."

A silence settled between us, and I decided to conclude the conversation. "Look, I need to go. I'm running late for rehearsal. Take care, Elise. I'll talk to you soon." I ended the call before she could delve deeper, as I had very few answers. Then I sank back onto the couch, closing my eyes, my mind consumed once again by thoughts of my assistant.

Ever since I kissed Caroline, I couldn't erase the taste of her lips from my memory. The sensation of her body trembling in my arms, accompanied by the soft moans that emanated from deep within her, played on a continuous loop. It didn't matter where I was or what I was doing; the recollection of that forbidden kiss haunted me. I forced my eyes open and hit the red-tassel pillow beside me.

That kiss should never have happened. I was Caroline's superior, and it wasn't fair of me to place her in such a position. But I couldn't resist, not when she looked at me with those eyes.

"Who am I kidding? I'm losing my mind over Caroline," I murmured, pushing myself up from the couch. It was nearly time for my daily ordeal at work, except today would be worse. During the dress rehearsal, Caroline would be constantly around me, applying my makeup and helping me change costumes swiftly between scenes. Until now, I could always find a reason to send Caroline out of the room if I needed to remove any clothing. But today was different. She'd be assisting with my costumes, touching my skin, driving me to the brink of insanity.

There was no way out of it, unless I spilled the beans to Peter or Bella. Told them I'd had a momentary loss of sanity, or confessed that I lacked all sense of self-control whenever Caroline was in my presence. If I did that, I wouldn't be disciplined or fired. I was the star soprano, after all. It would be Caroline who'd pay the price if I gave into temptation.

"That's not about to happen."

———

"You appear different, more refreshed," Caroline murmured as she applied moisturizer to my skin with her warm, soft hands. Damn it, the simple touch of her fingerss turned me on. I closed my eyes, hoping Caroline wouldn't notice. Once Caroline finished applying the cream, I heard her rummaging through her makeup kit. I opened my eyes and all I could see was her shapely ass inches away. I needed a distraction, so I hummed my character's aria from the second act of Cosi Fan Tutte. It exposed the fragility of love as the two main male characters disguised themselves as foreigners, seducing each other's girlfriends without being recognized, revealing the unrealistic nature of romantic love.

"I love that aria, even though I don't understand the lyrics," Caroline remarked, spinning around with a brush and makeup in hand. "Look up at the ceiling."

Caroline placed her hand on my bare shoulder for balance. I noticed her trembling hands and the dampness of her palm. As she applied makeup under my eyes, the brush quivered, and once again, my body reacted. The desire for Caroline overwhelmed me, but I knew I couldn't act on those feelings. It was torturous, as if I were paying for sins committed in a past life.

"Close your eyes, Maria," Caroline instructed, and I complied. For a moment, panic set in, and I struggled to breathe. My heart raced, unsure how much longer I could endure without taking her in my arms and tasting her lips once more. When Caroline finished, I took a deep breath. She gazed into my eyes without moving. There was a mixture of heat and desire in that look, and I couldn't look away.

"Maria, I..."

"No, don't say another word," I whispered, stepping in front of her. The brush slipped from her grasp and fell to the floor. I gently touched her cheek, and she flinched, prompting me to withdraw my hand.

"Don't touch me like that if you don't mean it," Caroline murmured, her eyes welling up with tears. The sensation of her flushed cheek lingered on the palm of my hand. I attempted to speak, to reassure her, but no words came out.

"This is driving me insane, Maria. You send mixed signals, and I know we shouldn't pursue this, but I..." Before she could utter another syllable, I grasped her shoulders and pulled Caroline into an embrace, nuzzling her neck. "No, I'm not sending mixed signals," I whispered in her ear, sensing her trembling response. "I'm burning with desire for you, Caroline." Then, I gently cupped her cheeks and kissed her lips. "There's nothing I want more than to taste you and hold you right now."

Caroline's knees weakened, and I steadied her by placing a hand on the small of her back. "Is this what you desire, Caroline? Because I can't resist touching you. You're driving me to madness. Each time I see you, I crave you. No one has ever evoked such feelings within me," I whispered breathlessly. Caroline responded by wrapping her arms around my waist, pulling me close. We locked eyes, and as our lips collided, my mind went blank.

Caroline's kiss tasted of mint, and her body trembled as our tongues intertwined. Her grip on me tightened, intensifying the passion and urgency of our embrace. Her hand trailed to my ass, squeezing gently. I pushed her back until she collided with the counter, causing brushes and cosmetics to cascade to the floor with a crash. Reluctantly, I pulled away from Caroline's lips and rested my forehead against hers.

"You..." I managed to utter, but before I could say more, there was a knock at the door. Our eyes widened, and I whispered, "Is the door locked?" Caroline nodded yes. I bent down to collect the fallen brushes and compacts, and the knocking persisted.

"Maria?"

Oh no, it was Bella.

"You need to let her in," I whispered, glancing at the mirror in the process. Damn, my lipstick was smudged.

"I'll be right there," Caroline called out, tossing me a white towel and hissing, "Sit!"

Caroline crossed the room and opened the door, while I arranged the towel over my bare shoulders. Bella stood motionless in the doorway, her inquisitive gaze taking in the scene. I noticed Caroline's cheeks turned beet red, and her usually sleek black hair was disheveled.

"Am I interrupting something?" Bella inquired, a mischievous smirk tugging at her lips.

"No, not at all, ma'am," Caroline stuttered, stepping back to allow Bella to enter. Bella sauntered in, and that's when I heard a sound akin to snapping wood. She bent down, wearing a puzzled expression, picked up a broken makeup brush from the floor, and handed it to Caroline with a wink. "Sorry about that."

———

Bella's words in the dressing room barely registered in my ears. It had something to do with my character and the scene where our fiancées confront us about our affairs. When she turned to leave, Bella's gaze shifted to Caroline, and a grin formed on her lips. "Keep up the good work."

We were now halfway through the second act of the dress rehearsal, and after an exhausting duet, I hurried offstage. I raised my arms, signaling to Caroline that it was time to remove my bodice. The fabric clung to my body, posing a challenge for her. Instead of moving on to my next costume, Caroline reached for a towel and began dabbing my sweaty torso.

"Do you always perspire this much?" Caroline whispered, causing a smile to curl on my lips.

"Only when you're near," I winked.

"Please, I need to concentrate," Caroline whispered back, tossing the damp towel onto a nearby table. She scanned our surroundings, noticing the makeup designer and another wardrobe attendant standing a few feet away. "Extend your arms," Caroline instructed, swiftly retrieving a new bodice and stepping onto a stool to help me put it on. Her fingers fumbled as she fastened the top buttons.

"Hurry," the other wardrobe attendant urged Caroline. "You have fifteen seconds."

Caroline swiftly swapped my wig with a fresh one. With little time to spare, I felt the moisture on my skin beneath the snug bodice.

"We'll continue what we started in the dressing room, Caroline. Your touch is driving me..." I began, but then my cue echoed through the air, and reluctantly, I dashed back onto the stage.

———

"Why didn't you join us after the rehearsal?" I asked, closing the dressing room door behind me. "I think Bella noticed your absence." Following the rehearsal, the theater had been filled with performers, musicians, and backstage crew as Peter and Bella provided us with notes.

Caroline's back was turned to me, her attention focused on the makeup brushes she was cleaning. She remained silent, neither turning around nor uttering a word. I approached her, gently placing my hands on her shoulders. Caroline glanced up, meeting my gaze through the mirror. Her eyes glistened, and I prayed it wasn't tears.

"I can't continue like this, Maria. One day you passionately kiss me, and the next you barely acknowledge my presence.

What will it be today? Will I receive the cold shoulder tomorrow, all because of the kiss we shared earlier?" Her voice trembled.

Leaning in, I nestled my lips against the nape of her neck. "I know we shouldn't be involved like this, Caroline, but whenever I see you, all I want to do is..." I turned her around, lightly brushing my lips against hers. "Kiss you. And so much more."

Caroline placed a quivering hand on my chest and let out a sigh. She opened her mouth to speak, but no words escaped. I gently lifted her chin with a finger, tilting her face upward, and whispered, "So, what happens now?"

CHAPTER

Fifteen

CAROLINE

THE PHONE in my apron vibrated, startling me. Thinking it could be Bella, I signaled to Maria and took it out, my stomach tied in knots. To my surprise, it was my personal phone, not the one provided by the Opera.

"Damn," I muttered, recognizing the caller. It was my ex-girlfriend Marilyn. Given the late hour, she was likely drunk, crying, or both. I noticed several unread messages from her in the past few days.

"Who is it? Bella?" Maria inquired.

"No, it's..." I placed the phone on the dressing room table, untied my apron, and draped it over the wooden director's chair. Maria rested her hand on my shoulder, her gaze intense. I yearned to reciprocate her touch, but memories of Kim firing me from Montaldo's swirled in my mind. I also feared that any new relationship would end up as turbulent as my previous one with Marilyn. Moreover, did I truly want to date someone who could terminate my employment on a whim? Placing my hand on Maria's, I gently removed it from my shoulder and interlaced our fingers.

"Maria, it's clear that I'm incredibly attracted to you, but I need some time to think," I confessed, my heart racing. Taking this risk meant requesting space to sort through my thoughts. It could be my only opportunity with her. What if she decided I wasn't worth the wait?

Maria's head dropped, and she looked up with an air of resignation. She pulled me into an embrace, holding me tightly as her heartbeat thumped against my chest. Then, she kissed my forehead and whispered, "I'll be here, waiting for you."

———

Instead of hailing an Uber, I opted to walk home. The night air felt refreshingly cool, with clear skies devoid of clouds. Being a brisk walker, the rhythmic sound of my sneakers meeting the pavement had a hypnotic effect. The almost full moon cast a haunting glow, and despite the partygoers stumbling out of nightclubs and restaurants on Peace Street, I felt alone with my thoughts.

"The most captivating woman I've ever known is an opera star, and she also happens to be my boss," I whispered. But my track record with lovers left much to be desired. Thoughts immediately turned to the unread text messages from Marilyn. Retrieving my personal phone from my back pocket, I halted, contemplating whether I should read them.

Ah, to hell with it. If she's blowing up my phone like this, it must be important. I leaned against the brick wall of a nearby restaurant. A dirty orange alley cat streaked across the sidewalk, chased by another feline, startling me. Walking home at this late hour perhaps wasn't the wisest choice.

I clicked on the first unopened message Marilyn had sent a week and a half ago.

Went to my first AA meeting today

"About time," I muttered, proceeding to the next message.

Can I call you? I need to talk about something

Due to my constant work commitments, I'd largely ignored my personal phone. Glancing at my call log, I noticed Marilyn's repeated attempts to reach me in the past few days. It struck me that if Maria hadn't monopolized my attention, I might have responded to her messages. In fact, I might have even met up with her, hoping to support her sudden onset of sobriety. After our breakup, when asked about the end of our relationship, my usual response would be that Marilyn had an affair with Jose Cuervo, choosing tequila over me. She was a messy drunk who once caused a fire in our house when she attempted to cook hot dogs in the middle of the night. Marilyn had passed out at the kitchen table while the hot dogs and the wall behind them turned to ashes. That incident had been the final straw, and I moved out two days later. Yet, despite everything, I continued dating her out of fear that she might harm herself while drunk. Opening the next message, dated four days ago, I read:

I know you hate me

"Fucker," I whispered, gazing up at the moon as a tear slid down my cheek. I could never truly hate her. Marilyn possessed a boundless heart. It was her drinking problem that forced me to end our relationship.

My finger hovered over the next message, but instead, I stashed the phone back into my pocket. Wiping away the tears from my face, I had an epiphany. These tears weren't solely about the loss of my relationship with Marilyn. They represented the culmination of pent-up tension that had been building ever since I first started working for Maria.

For some time now, a timid voice in my head had urged me to let go of the past and embrace an uncertain future. This meant relinquishing the all-too-familiar emotions I once harbored for Marilyn. Although I knew it was the best decision for my sanity, it proved incredibly challenging. I wasn't in love with Marilyn anymore; that flame was long gone. But the idea of moving forward paralyzed me.

Shaking off my thoughts, I pushed myself off the wall and resumed my homeward journey.

The light was red at the corner of Peace Street and 1st. I would've crossed it against the light, but several cars from the Flex bar parking lot were pulling out onto the street. Maybe a cocktail would help me sleep?

When the light turned green I crossed 1st Street, and turned to cross Peace to go to Flex when the sight of a familiar face stopped me in my tracks.

Marilyn was stumbling out of Steward's, a restaurant next door to Flex. Her olive skin shone under the streetlight, and she looked far too skinny to be healthy. A tall, younger girl with blond hair was next to her, and they were both laughing. Marilyn's hip hit the sandwich board sign on the sidewalk displaying the nightly specials at Flex, and the blond girl threw her arm around Marilyn's shoulders to steady her. Then the girl held the door to the bar open, and they went inside, Marilyn's feet tripping over the top step as the door shut behind them. I spun around and walked in the opposite direction, surprised that I felt nothing but relief. Or was it numbness?

Didn't matter. Marilyn was no longer my problem.

———

"Well, this is quite a surprise," Catrina remarked from across the bar, her lips adorned with that flawless shade of red she always wore.

"After a tough day at work, I figured I'd have a nightcap before hitting the sack. Can I get a..." I paused for a moment, knowing exactly what I wanted. "...a pint of beer and a shot of Cuervo."

The craving for a drink had intensified during my walk home, and when I stumbled upon Catrina's bar, I decided to step in for a quick one. It felt almost rebellious. When I was with Marilyn, I was always the sober one, ensuring her safe return home. Catrina's place was mostly empty, with just a few NC State students playing pool. I was the lone customer at the bar, and I wondered if it was close to closing time. Glancing at my phone, I realized it was almost midnight and mentally reminded myself to head home after this round. I had to be at work by ten and didn't want to feel rough in the morning.

"Here you go, sweetie," Catrina placed the drinks and a finger bowl of limes in front of me. "That stuff is addictive." She chuckled, pointing at the tequila, and I joined in. I was all too aware of just how addictive it could be.

"So, how's the job treating you? I keep seeing the singer you work for all over social media. Have you figured out which team she plays for?" All thoughts of my ex evaporated from my mind, instantly replaced by the memory of Maria's arms tightly wrapped around my waist. I had decisions to make and wondered if I was even in the right state of mind to tackle them.

"Knock knock," Catrina rapped her knuckles on the bar to regain my attention. "Are you doing okay, Caroline?"

"Oh, sorry, I was..." I gestured towards my head, then picked up the shot glass and a lime wedge. "Cheers." I downed the tequila and winced at its sharp taste. I couldn't fathom how

Marilyn drank so much of it. Then, I recollected how Maria hardly drank anything other than warm water and herbal tea.

A point in Maria's favor.

"Well, tell me all about your boss. She's a stunning woman," Catrina glanced momentarily at the pool table before refocusing on me. I took a sip of my beer, then pushed the empty shot glass across the bar and nodded.

"Maria's the reason I had such a rough day," I sighed, and Catrina promptly refilled my glass, placing it back in front of me. "What happened? Was she behaving like a diva or something?" Before I could reply, one of the students at the pool table called out Catrina's name, holding up an empty beer pitcher. "Be right back."

As she left, I pondered whether I could trust her. She knew Bella and Lilith, and I definitely didn't want this conversation getting back to them. However, I needed someone to talk to, and bartenders were often great listeners. She didn't know me well, which meant she might offer a more objective viewpoint.

"Alright, spill the beans. What's going on with your boss?" Catrina stood in front of me again, her arms crossed over her chest. She wore a black tank top with jeans, and it seemed like tattoos covered every inch of her. Leaning back on the barstool, I contemplated whether I should confide in her, when suddenly, her eyebrows lifted and a mischievous smile spread across her face.

"You've got a crush on her, don't you?" she teased.

I propped my elbows on the bar, burying my face in my hands, and groaned. "You can't tell anyone, okay?"

"Don't worry, your secret's safe with me. I can't blame you, though. That woman looks like a movie star. Every time I ride the elevator with her in our building, I have to resist the urge to stare," she said, and I couldn't help but giggle. Soon, a wave of laughter surged through me, and I found myself slapping the bar with one hand while clutching my stomach with the other. It felt like all the tension in my body had burst out, and the laughter seemed unstoppable. Tears welled up in my eyes, and as the laughter gradually subsided, I looked across the bar to see Catrina also giggling. Now my stomach ached, and I questioned whether I could handle the second shot of tequila sitting before me.

"So, what's so funny, Caroline? I mean, anyone who lays eyes on that woman is bound to..." Catrina began.

"You won't believe it," I interrupted, then tossed back the second shot. This time, it went down smoothly, no need for a lime. I slammed the glass back on the bar. "We kissed. I mean, we really kissed each other."

Catrina gasped, and our eyes locked.

"Hahahahaha!"

I couldn't help but feel overwhelmed by the absurdity of the situation. Why would someone as talented and attractive as Maria be interested in someone like me? I'd spent most of my career in menial retail jobs, and my love life had been a series of disasters.

"Caroline, most people would be ecstatic if a woman like that made a move on them. So why are you..." Catrina started, but I interrupted her with a raised hand.

"Because Maria is my boss. Not only that, she's the star of the show. If we were to get involved, it would jeopardize my position, not hers. Besides, it's just bad timing," I explained, biting my lower lip as thoughts of Marilyn and the blonde girl she was with earlier invaded my mind.

"What do you mean by bad timing? I understand the professional boundaries, but timing?" Catrina grabbed a shot glass and poured tequila for both of us. We clinked our glasses together and downed the shots. I covered my glass with a napkin, signaling I didn't want another.

"I ran into my ex today. Well, not exactly. I saw her entering Flex with another girl, and it's making me question if I'm ready for something serious right now," I confessed.

"How long have you been broken up?" Catrina inquired.

"Three years," I replied.

Catrina's eyes widened in surprise. "Three years? And you're still hung up on her?"

"No, that's the messed-up part. I'm not in love with her at all. It's just... our relationship was incredibly dysfunctional. Marilyn has a severe drinking problem, and it made me realize that I may have enabled her behavior. I'm genuinely afraid of getting involved with anyone else. It feels safer to hide away in my apartment because I don't trust myself with women. Every person I've dated has had some serious issues. Now that Maria has shown interest, I can't help but wonder what's wrong with her. It's like normal, stable women are repelled by me," I confessed, my voice trembling. I wiped away tears with the back of my hand and sniffed.

"Caroline, I think you're selling yourself short. Everyone has their issues; they just hide them. Imagine if your favorite movie star posted the reality of their life on Instagram instead of the fake facade. Nobody is genuinely open about their problems," Catrina reassured me, placing her hand on mine and giving it a comforting squeeze. "If anything, you have an advantage with Maria. You work with her every day and probably know her better than anyone else. And let me tell you something else. You shouldn't be as worried about her being your boss as you are. Bella and Lilith met at the symphony, and trust me, nobody batted an eye when they got together."

"But…"

"Maria is attracted to you for a reason, and it seems to me like it's mutual, right?" Catrina asked. I nodded, opened my mouth to speak, but she cut me off.

"I understand your concerns about the boss/employee thing, but there are ways to work around it. Just talk to the woman and set up some boundaries of your own. And as far as your ex goes..." Catrina walked to the end of the bar, pulled a picture frame from the wall and returned. She glanced over it, then showed it to me. At the top of it in bold letters it said MOST WANTED. Then she pointed at a very familiar face.

"Is this your ex, um, let's see here, Marilyn Hernandez?"

I groaned, then muttered, "Yes. How do you know..."

"This is our list of people we've banned from the bar for violating the rules. According to this note, she threw a punch at a bartender after being cut off. It's time for you to move on, Caroline, because you deserve a helluva lot better than this girl." Catrina placed the frame to the side and then took my hand in hers.

"Take a chance on Maria. What have you got to lose?"

CHAPTER
Sixteen

MARIA

"WHERE WAS CAROLINE AFTER REHEARSAL?" Lilith asked. I shrugged and said nothing, unwilling to put Caroline in trouble with Bella, who walked on Lilith's other side. We were the last ones to exit the rehearsal hall, our footsteps echoing in the grimy parking deck.

Usually, I would have been among the first to leave. However, after Caroline hurried away, I found myself sitting in my dressing room, pondering what I had done to scare her off. It was evident that she was as attracted to me as I was to her. The difference was, I had grown tired of fighting a losing battle. Despite the professional circumstances we faced, I believed there had to be a way to make something work between us.

"Tell Caroline to email Peter for any necessary notes." Bella muttered, opening the trunk of her Jaguar for Lilith to store her cello. "Also, make sure she understands that attending all future meetings is mandatory." As the trunk slammed shut, a flicker of concern for Caroline stirred within me.

"Of course,, Bella,' I muttered, promptly entering my Mercedes and closing the door before she could say anything more. A moment later, Bella reversed from her parking spot and sped towards the ramp, tires screeching. I turned my head to observe, only to witness Lilith's eyes widen in terror. Bella had to be the worst driver I had ever seen. I couldn't comprehend why Lilith allowed her to take the wheel.

I rubbed the back of my neck, shut my eyes, and sank into the plush leather seat. The memory of Caroline's lips lingered, and a wave of desire surged through me. My assistant was driving me to distraction, and what made it more challenging was knowing that she felt the same way. Yet, Caroline had every reason to fear me.

'Damn it,' I muttered, then turned the key in the ignition. 'Somehow, some way, I will make you mine, Caroline Frank.'"

———

The air in my study was humid, thanks to the humidifier, and my skin felt sticky. After completing my nightly workout of squats, push-ups, and stretches, I collapsed onto the overstuffed blue sofa I had purchased from a local antique store. I had never been one for shopping, but lately, I needed to keep busy when I wasn't at work. The original plan had been for Caroline to handle most of that stuff. However, for the last few weeks, I had kept her away from the apartment, hoping the attraction I felt for her would die down.

It hadn't worked.

"Damn it," I moaned, slipping my hand under my shorts. I had never been a big fan of masturbating. Usually, it bored me, but lately, I had been feeling the urge, and it made being around Caroline easier. I gently rubbed myself through the thin fabric of my black panties, feeling the material grow damper with every second.

This desire started when she had spent the afternoon with

me, eating that delicious soup she had made. Something inside of me just turned on, like a light switch. Since then, I noticed everything about her. Caroline's magnificent eyes and that round ass that teased me whenever she turned around. I wanted to taste her heat and run my hands through...

The phone rang.

"Who the hell is calling so late?" I complained to the empty room. According to the simple black and white clock on the opposite wall, it was two thirty in the morning. "Something might be wrong," I muttered, then with a start, realized it could be Caroline. I leapt to my feet, raced across the room, and grabbed my phone off of the desk. When I saw who it was, my shoulders dropped, and I sighed.

"Elise. Are you okay? It's very early here." Italy was five hours ahead, so it was only seven thirty in the morning there.

"Sorry, did I wake you? It's just... I had this dream. Damn. I shouldn't have called, but I woke up worried about you."

The opera world was tiny and extremely competitive. I had rarely allowed myself the luxury of friendships with people in the business, except for Elise. If it had been just about anyone else on the line, I wouldn't have answered the call, so I knew she must be upset about something.

"Sweetheart, I'm fine," I reassured. "Don't worry about me." I sat in the leather chair behind the desk and sighed.

"You don't sound good. Is it the upcoming production?" she asked.

"No, I'm... just going through some personal stuff. Cosi fan Tutte will do very well, and as you've noted before, I know the role of Despina inside and out."

Silence hung between us for a moment, and then she let out a lengthy sigh. "You don't have to tell me what's wrong, but I feel it from across the ocean. Maria, you are not only my pupil, but also one of my dearest friends. Please, if there is something wrong, you can confide in me."

Pressure built behind my eyes, and it all came spilling out, as if she were a priest taking my confession.

"...And then I pushed her away, like a fool. But I have no experience with relationships. Caroline scared me so..."

"Caroline doesn't scare you," Elise interrupted. "Your feelings do. I've always wondered why a woman gifted with your immense talent and looks remained alone. I'm not trying to inflate your ego, Maria, but you could have any woman, or man for that matter, that you wanted," she said, and I thought I detected a hint of bitterness. I cocked my head, wondering if what I had suspected about her feelings for me was true.

"Caroline is your employee, correct?"

"Yes, well, technically she works for the opera, but I'm her boss."

"That girl has a lot to lose if things were to go sour between you, doesn't she?" she asked. I heard a tea kettle whistling from across the Atlantic Ocean. "Excuse me, Maria. I'll be right back."

I wasn't totally clueless about the situation, and Elise was right. Caroline had a lot more to lose than I did. But I knew I'd never deliberately harm the younger woman.

"You need to set clear boundaries with Caroline because you're not the only one who's scared. Reassure her that no matter what happens between the two of you, she will come to no harm, at least as far as her job is concerned," Elise sighed. "It would be best if you steer clear of the entire situation. I want nothing but happiness for you, but dating your assistant can lead you down dangerous paths, Maria. Let me ask you something," she asked, and I grunted in reply. "Is Caroline worth the potential upheaval she could cause you? Do you want to risk losing the career you've fought so hard to regain?"

―――――――

Dark circles stared back at me in the mirrored walls of the elevator. I had tossed and turned for a few hours but finally gave up on trying to get proper sleep at 10 a.m. and headed downstairs to the gym on the first floor to sweat the bullshit out of my head.

The elevator stopped on the eighth floor, and a woman I had seen a few times around the building got on. She was an exotic creature, with wavy black hair, bright red lips, and colorful tattoos covering her body.

"Hi," she stuck her hand out. "I'm Catrina. My brother Frank owns the building, and I live here too. I see you around occasionally and thought I'd introduce myself."

I took her hand in mine and gave it a quick squeeze. "Maria Wagner. It's a pleasure."

Not in the mood to encourage conversation, I pulled my phone out of the pocket of my hoodie and pretended to check my emails.

"I know who you are."

I glanced in her direction. She was smirking.

"Oh really? Well, I'm at a disadvantage, I'm afraid."

"You're Caroline Frank's boss. She's a friend of mine, and..." The doors opened on the ground floor, and I gestured for her to exit first. "...well, it was nice meeting you. Maybe next time we can chat over drinks or something." The woman gave a cheery wave and raced out of the building before I could reply. I laughed to myself, then realized that Caroline had been talking about me to someone. It felt strange and almost unwelcome until it hit me that with her smirks and sideways glances, she must have been discussing me in a not-so-professional way.

With a bounce in my step, I punched in the code for the gym on the small keypad and let myself in. To my dismay, Bella was pedaling away on a bicycle, listening to something on her phone. When she saw me, she removed her earbuds and grinned.

"Ready for opening night tonight?"

I wasn't there to ride a bicycle in place, but I didn't want to ignore my conductor while working on the weights, so I climbed onto the bike next to hers.

"As ready as I'll ever be. So, what brings you here? I didn't know you lived in the building," I said, then began to pedal.

"I used to live here, but Frank and I are friends, and he lets me and some of his other friends use the gym. He's a cool guy. I'd say get to know him, but he's working on a building project in Norfolk at the moment, and hardly any of us see much of him right now." Bella pulled her water bottle out of the holder on the handles and took a drink. "So, as long as I have your undivided attention, let me ask you something."

My fingers tightened on the bike handles. "Sure."

"Is Caroline doing a good job?"

My feet stopped pumping the pedals for a moment, then I forced them to move again.

"Yes, of course she is. Caroline is an excellent assistant, and I, um, like her..."

"That's excellent to hear because I'd swear I felt some tension between the two of you and wondered if she was staying on top of things. When she didn't show up for the cast meeting after rehearsal last night, I..."

"Caroline wasn't feeling well, that's all," I cut Bella off before she could delve further into that line of thinking. "I have nothing but praise for Caroline's performance. She has definitely made my job easier, allowing me to focus on what's important: the music. Plus, she, um, is on top of everything. I never expected to have such an amazing personal assistant. Caroline is a model employee." I had to restrain myself from gushing too much, but I had to reassure Bella that there was nothing wrong with Caroline.

Bella quit pedaling, threw her hands up in mock surrender, and laughed.

"I get it! Caroline is perfect in her job." Bella chuckled, and instead of turning toward her, I glanced at our reflections in the floor-to-ceiling mirrored wall in front of us. She took another swig of water and climbed off the bike, her eyes never leaving mine in the mirror.

"Hey, did I ever tell you about how I met Lilith?" Bella asked, wiping her forehead with a white towel.

"No," I murmured and realized I had stopped pedaling. Instead of addressing her reflection, I turned toward her. "Why do you want to...?"

"I met her at a coffee shop up the street called The Morning Vibe." Bella interrupted and paced in front of me. "The first time I laid eyes on her, I knew there was something between us. Then, on my first day of rehearsals, I discovered she played the cello for the symphony. Imagine my surprise." Bella walked toward the door. It looked like she would leave without saying another word. I couldn't let her leave without telling me how she worked around the problem of being Lilith's boss.

"So what happened? You didn't feel there was an issue with...?"

"Issues? My only issue was getting her to say yes. Damn, that girl played hard to get." Bella winked, then walked out the door.

CHAPTER
Seventeen

CAROLINE

INSTEAD OF PERIOD COSTUMES, our stage director had chosen a contemporary style, which made my job much easier. Instead of dealing with layers of ruffles and breeches from the eighteenth century, Maria would wear modern clothing that was much easier to work with for quick costume changes. That was the only straightforward thing I had to deal with on opening night, because the star of the show apparently wasn't speaking, and I was a nervous mess.

Maria had reverted to writing everyone notes again. She sent me a text earlier asking me to inform Peter and Bella about this precautionary measure. That was all she texted. She didn't mention a word about last night. Maria claimed she had a tickle in the back of her throat and wanted to be extra careful with her voice. Bella had been in Maria's dressing room when she arrived, and when Maria handed her a note, Bella rolled her eyes.

"You do whatever it takes to keep that instrument in good working order." Bella said condescendingly and patted Maria on the shoulder. Then Bella threw her arm around me and loudly whispered, "She's such a diva."

Maria's nostrils flared, and Bella barked out a laugh.

"I'm kidding! You're going to be fantastic tonight, I just know it. Now, I've got to run along and herd the musicians into their seats. *Toi toi toi*, Maria!" And with that, Bella rushed out.

We stood and stared at each other, neither of us moving a muscle. It was like time stood still, waiting for one of us to say or do something. My knees felt weak, and a sensation of warmth filled my chest. I wanted to launch myself into her arms, but the fear of rejection held me back. Though I was the one who'd asked for more time to think things through, I feared Maria might have changed her mind about me. What if she wanted to keep it strictly professional? In my head I knew that was the smartest thing to do, but my heart was screaming for so much more.

Finally, Maria moved, hanging her jacket on the clothes rack. I cleared my throat and turned toward the makeup counter, pulling my brushes out of their case and lining them up.

I heard Maria moving around behind me. The sound of her fingers fumbling with the buttons of her blouse, and her heels being kicked off and pushed to the side. I desperately wanted to turn around, to watch the slow striptease she always made before sending me out of the dressing room in search of warm water. I was wet, not even needing to see her. Her lavender citrus scent invaded my nostrils, and I inhaled deeply, and then without thinking I glanced into the mirror, hoping to catch a glimpse of her without being caught.

I gasped. Maria was behind me, staring at my reflection in the mirror, wearing nothing at all.

"Caroline," Maria breathed, then placed her hand on my shoulder, "after the show, we must talk."

We only had half an hour until the curtain went up. I was all fingers and thumbs while applying her makeup, continuously dropping brushes and sponges while avoiding her eyes. If I were to stare into them, it would've paralyzed me. As it was, I could barely breathe. Every time my fingers touched her skin I felt little electric shocks, and it didn't help that she was sitting in my makeup chair wearing nothing but a towel. Now I understood why she'd always sent me from the room so she could change into her costume. Seeing her completely naked was a revelation. Maria's body was both feminine and athletic, her arms and legs perfectly sculpted. I wanted to lick her unblemished porcelain skin, and run my hands across her taut stomach.

"Look up to the ceiling." I whispered, then with my trembling ring finger I dabbed concealer under her left eye. When I finished with that one and was about to move to the other, her gaze dropped, locking with mine. Maria's eyes were wet and soft, and I could detect a hint of red blossoming on her cheeks underneath the heavy pancake makeup. She swallowed, and stupid me shifted my gaze down to her chest. Her breasts were perfect, though the towel she wore partially hid them. Suddenly, I couldn't breathe. I leaned back against the counter, shut my eyes and willed myself to act vaguely normal.

"Do you see what you are doing to me?" Maria whispered. "How am I going to sing when all I can think of is how much I want to touch you, to feel your flesh burning underneath me while I..."

The phone pinged in my apron pocket.

"Fuck me." I whimpered.

"Exactly." Maria licked her lips, and a shiver raced down my spine.

I pulled the phone from my apron and noted the time. It was an alarm I'd set to make sure Maria was running on schedule. She had only ten more minutes to be ready. The way things were going, she would hit the stage with jacked-up makeup in her birthday suit.

"We only have a few more minutes before you go on stage." I croaked, then jammed my phone back into the apron. Maria reached for me, and I knew if she had her way she'd never make it in time. I pushed back against her shoulders and held her still.

"After the show. We'll finish this."

Maria grabbed my wrist and growled, "Damn right we will."

———

The opening scene of the opera had Maria's character Despina and the other female leads sitting in a lounge, gossiping about their boyfriends. None of them believed in love, or a man's ability to be faithful. Since I was backstage and couldn't see the subtitles, I didn't know exactly what they were singing about. Considering the fact that my ex-girlfriend had been what I liked to call a *woman of easy virtue*, I could understand their characters' skepticism. Faithlessness was much more common than fidelity.

I'd heard Maria practice many times before, but now that she was before a live audience, it was a totally different experience. She gave it her all, and what truly amazed me was that her voice filled a two-thousand-seat theater without a microphone, and on top of a full orchestra. I used to marvel at the abilities of pop singers like Whitney and Mariah, but they couldn't hold a candle to a trained opera singer like Maria. It was like comparing Burger King to a five star Parisian restaurant.

What really held me enthralled was her acting ability. On top of singing an insane amount of notes and being heard by thousands of people with no other amplification than her throat, the energy she brought to the role was incredible. Something changed in the color of her voice that moved me, and she could perform vocal acrobatics all while moving and dancing around the stage. For a regular pop star to do that they'd either lip sync or use a microphone. It also explained why she was covered in sweat during rehearsals, because it was an awesome physical endeavor to do what she did on that stage.

"I brought an bodice and hung it on Maria's rack, just in case." One of the wardrobe supervisors whispered in my ear, startling me. "One more minute. Are you ready?"

I nodded and snatched a terry cloth hand towel off the stack on the table next to me. Then I shut my eyes and steadied my breathing. Now was not the time to lose my professional composure. Seconds later, I heard applause, then the sound of footsteps rushing toward me and opened my eyes.

Maria stood before me with her arms outstretched. Instead of buttons on the cuffs they were held together by velcro, so I yanked them open, then I pulled at her shirt collar, which was also held in place by velcro, then lifted the sopping wet blouse over her head and threw it aside. Maria was drenched in sweat, and I grabbed a towel and began mopping her off before putting her next shirt on.

Her familiar lavender and citrus scent filled my head, and I felt lightheaded. I almost fell into her, but caught myself in the nick of time by placing my free hand on her shoulder for balance. Maria grabbed my wrist, and a guttural moan vibrated through her chest. I couldn't hear it because of the performers on stage, but I felt it move up my arm then down to my pussy.

"Maria, please." I breathed, and our eyes locked.

She leaned forward and licked the skin under my ear, then whispered, "Baby, let's get through this performance, because tonight I will make you mine."

CHAPTER

Eighteen

MARIA

I WALKED OFF THE STAGE, my heart a whirlwind of emotions – anticipation, elation, and a healthy dose of fear. The applause had been deafening; I could feel the cracks of energy in the air, reverberating like rolling thunder that made it impossible to turn away.

I heard the gasps of surprise and admiration from the audience as I hit my last note, and I knew I had delivered a performance my vocal coach Elise would be proud of.

"You were magnificent!" Angela exclaimed, throwing her arms around my shoulders. I winced, not because she'd touched me, but because of the other performers crammed into my dressing room. Every face held a mixture of admiration and envy, and it made me feel both proud and uncomfortable in equal measure. A few of them glanced down at the floor. I might be the star soprano, but everyone connected to this production deserved credit for the fabulous show we put on tonight.

"Thank you." I murmured, then backed away from the

Human Resources manager. "The entire cast made this the most memorable Cosi Fan Tutte I've ever performed in. Cheers!" I lifted the champagne glass from the makeup counter and brought it to my lips, then set it down again without drinking any of it. Caroline was across the room typing into her phone while the stage director Peter yammered away in her ear, most likely giving Carolyn notes about my performance which I would read in the morning.

The door to the dressing room flung open and Bella strolled in with Lilith a step behind her. The backstage crew and singers moved back to let the conductor have the center of the room. There was a buzz of excitement, like bees circling around a hive. Lilith stood next to Peter and Caroline, who were still conferring. They paused when Bella clapped her hands several times for silence.

"Thanks to all of you for an incredible performance this evening. As all of you know, our Raleigh performances sold out, but Greensboro and Charlotte have seen slower ticket sales. I just heard from Greta Dollitz, the reviewer from the Charlotte NPR station WFAE. She loved the show. And, instead of just running the review on the local station, Greta will run a story nationally about the performance. I predict not only sold-out performances of this opera, but for the rest of the season!"

The room erupted into applause as Bella announced the news of our success. Everyone was beaming, and for a moment I forgot all my worries.

But then I looked towards Caroline and Peter, who were standing on the side of the room, and the reality came crashing back down. Peter was clapping wildly while Caroline stood still with her arms crossed at her sides. As soon as our eyes met, I felt a wave of heat rush up from my neck to my cheeks. All I wanted was for everyone to leave so I could talk to her alone.

"Well done, everyone!" Bella said over the noise, clapping one more time before departing with Lilith in tow. As soon as they left, the room became quieter and several of the singers began trickling out as well.

I sighed heavily and turned to watch Caroline typing on her phone, then she stopped and turned towards me. We were now alone in the dressing room, and a bizarre sense of awkwardness filled me.

"You were amazing out there tonight," she said softly, making my heart skip a beat even though we had been around each other for weeks now. "I knew you'd do great." She smiled sadly, then began to pack up her supplies. Without thinking, I stepped forward, placing my hand on her shoulder. She slowly turned toward me, and silently we eyed each other. I placed a hand on each side of her face, then realized I was still in my sweat soaked costume.

"I want you so damn bad, Caroline. But, if you can't tell, I must get cleaned up first. I'm sure I smell…"

The door to the dressing room flew open, and instead of jumping apart, Caroline and I slowly turned toward the intruder.

"Sorry, to interrupt." Bella said, suppressing a grin. "I forgot to tell the two of you that Greta wants to conduct a brief interview with us to use on her radio show. You must be there too, Caroline. It's tomorrow at 1:30 p.m. She's booked a small studio at the Raleigh NPR station, WCVE. She'll email Caroline the questions this evening so you'll be prepared." Bella turned around to leave. She shut the door halfway, then poked her head back in the dressing room. "You might want to lock this door. Just saying."

———

Neither of us spoke on the drive back to my place. When I passed Caroline's street she didn't say a word, though a fluttering of fear passed through me, thinking she might want to be dropped off at her place. Caroline squeezed my hand, then let it go so I could pull into the parking lot of my building. She was gazing at me with those intense eyes, and I felt my stomach fill with butterflies once again.When I turned the car off, I turned to her and placed my palm on the back of her neck.

"I've been waiting for this moment for so long, it feels…" I began, but Caroline placed her index finger over my lips, and I felt a spark of electricity spark between us. We looked deeply into each other's eyes for what seemed like hours, until finally Caroline leaned forward and softly pressed her lips against mine. It was just a brief kiss; yet it felt like the entire universe had stopped spinning just for us.

For a few moments we just held each other in silence, neither of us wanting to break the beautiful moment that had just passed between us. Finally Caroline pulled away slightly and looked down at her hands shyly before speaking:

"So...What now?"

"I'm terrified of messing this up, but you should know that this is a moment I've waited for my entire life." My breath hitched, and Caroline leaned foreward, resting her forehead against mine.

"Upstairs. Now." Caroline hissed, pushing the car door open.

We raced into the building, and when we both stepped into the elevator, I felt my hunger growing with each passing second. Every time I glanced at her she seemed to blush a bit darker, embarrassed by my stares of longing. The air in the elevator was charged with tension, and neither of us wanted to be the first one to break it.

For a moment I forgot to breathe, and a wave of dizziness

passed through me. When the doors slid open in front of my apartment, Caroline walked out and I stayed back and watched her move. Every step she took toward my door, and closer to my bed, I grew more excited. Caroline stood with her back to me for a beat, then she turned around with a raised eyebrow.

"Are you coming inside?" She asked. The elevator doors began to shut, and I rushed out.

"Sorry," I stammered, my cheeks burning in embarrassment. "I, I couldn't help myself, just um, watching you." Then I stuffed my hand in my pocket and yanked out the keys with unsteady fingers. When I went to insert the key in the lock, they fell to the floor. Caroline bent down and picked them up, and I felt her fingers trembling when she placed the keys in my hand.

She stepped aside so I could open the door and then followed me inside. The air felt charged with electricity as we stood facing each other for a moment in silence.

Finally Caroline broke the silence by asking, "So... what do you want to do now?" The question hung in the air between us like a heavy fog.

I swallowed hard and said, "Well...." before trailing off. My mind was spinning with thoughts of all the possibilities that were about to unfold before us.

"Before we take things any further I must get naked and wet," I winked. Caroline's gaze shifted down, and once again her cheeks burned red. "I mean I need to take a quick shower." I closed the distance between us and kissed her forehead. "After tonight's performance I smell like a barn animal."

"No," Caroline wrapped her fingers around the back of my neck. "You smell delicious, like lavender and oranges. It was one of the first things I noticed about you." She sighed, then brushed her lips over mine. "But if you want some company in the shower, I'd love to join you."

My heart skipped a beat. Caroline seemed to read my mind and knew exactly what I wanted.

Without saying another word, I took her hand and we moved towards the bathroom. As we passed through my bedroom, Caroline hesitated for a moment.

"Are you sure this is what you want?" I whispered. Caroline's lips trembled, then she pulled me toward the bathroom. When she opened the door, she dropped my hand and without a word unbuttoned her blouse, tossing it to the floor. She turned and I unhooked her bra, letting it fall on the blouse.

"This is taking so long," I muttered, then moved past her, sliding the glass doors to the shower open and turning on the hot water. In a matter of seconds my clothes were on the floor, and I kicked them away and turned to face Caroline. She was completely naked, and at the sight of her my pussy clenched.

"You're so beautiful," I murmured, "Like an angel."

Caroline's raven black hair curled slightly in the damp air as steam filled the bathroom. I stepped forward, brushing her hair off of her forehead. Caroline tilted her head, and I kissed her. Our lips moved together in perfect harmony as if they'd done this a million times before. The kiss deepened as I pulled Caroline closer to me, and she moaned softly in response. I explored the curves of her body with my hands and felt the warmth radiating off of every inch of her. Finally, I broke the kiss, took her hand, and pulled Caroline into the shower.

"I dreamed of this since the first day we met," Caroline whispered. "Kiss me again."

"Anything you want," I pulled her into me and our lips met again. The kiss deepened as I pulled Caroline closer to me, and she moaned softly in response. The water cascaded around us and the heat built up between us like a furnace, making it hard to breathe or think. Caroline pulled away for just a moment, then spun around to face the showerhead, pressing herself against me as the hot water ran down our bodies. She reached back with one hand, grasping my hip tightly as she angled her head up for another passionate kiss. Our skins felt glued together, all softness and curves. I felt her fingers on the curve of my breast and my grip on her tightened. Moist heat radiated from between my legs, then with a ragged gasp Caroline stepped back.

"Sit," She gestured toward the marble shower seat. "I must taste you."

My legs were trembling so much I nearly slid off the seat. Caroline straddled my lap, and a moment later her lips were attached to the soft skin under my ear.

"It would be so easy to become lost in you," I moaned, arching my back at the sensations. Caroline groaned in response, then she slid down my body until she was kneeling on the shower floor in front of me.

"Open," She whispered, placing a hand on each of my knees. Caroline pushed my legs apart, peppering little kisses up my thigh. In the moist heat of the shower I smelled my excitement, and it felt like I was on fire. My head fell back against the wall and I shut my eyes. Caroline's hand pressed against my clit, which pulsed at her touch.

"Please," I heard myself mutter. "Please, I need you so badly."

Her fingers glided between my legs until they encountered my wetness.

"This is a dream come true," Caroline said, then I felt her fingers circle my entrance. I spread my legs wider and felt a finger slip inside. Between the hot water raining down on us, and her fingers inside of me I was blazing with heat. She pushed her finger deeper inside me, then I felt her mouth on my clit.

"Yes," I gasped, feeling my aching bud pulse some more.

Caroline's mouth and fingers moved rhythmically, and each thrust brought me closer to the edge. Sensing my body's response, she stopped moving.

"The water's getting cold, Maria."

"What, oh, uh..."

Caroline got to her feet, turned off the water and took my hand. "Come on. Let's take this to bed."

CHAPTER
Nineteen

CAROLINE

NEVER IN MY wildest dreams did I believe Maria wanted me. She was glamorous and chic, while I was the exact opposite. But now she was mine, at least for a night. My heart raced as we walked into her bedroom, our skins still damp from the shower. This was our first time together, and in my fantasies we made love in her bed, falling asleep afterwards in each others arms.

At the foot of the bed Maria opened her arms. "Kiss me, Caroline."

I didn't need to be asked twice. I stepped closer, savoring the sweet scent of her skin mixed with the musk of our excitement. She sighed into my mouth as we kissed and I felt her knee press up into my clit. Her hard nipples pressed against mine, and a deep guttural moan came from deep within me.

Everything felt wet. Our skins, hair, and of course, my pussy was drenched with longing. The cavernous bedroom echoed with the sounds of our wet limbs, punctuated by kisses, and groans.

"Get on the bed," Maria ordered breathlessly, and I fell back on the mattress. She straddled my waist and pinched both of my nipples, her dark eyes never leaving mine. I whimpered, a sound I'd never made before in my life. "I can smell your excitement, and now I'm going to taste it."

Maria shifted, then slid down my body with my right leg in between hers. "I'm falling for you, Caroline."

A tear slid down my cheek, and I prayed she didn't see it. I wasn't the type of girl that good things happen to, and I didn't want her to be frightened by my feelings.

"Hey, don't cry." Maria moved up my body, pressing it against mine. She kissed my tears away, and I suppressed a sob. "Being with you is the best thing that's ever happened to me," she said softly. "And I hope you feel the same."

"I do, but…"

Maria kissed me, and I completely forgot what I was about to say. I felt her hand slide down my stomach, and I automatically thrust my hips up. A finger glanced over my clit, then slid down my lips, teasing me. Her mouth left mine, sliding across my cheek until they were on my neck, causing me to gasp.

"You like that," Maria whispered, and I felt her fingers back on my clit while she licked and sucked on my neck. Why on earth did Maria choose me?

Every feeling of inadequacy hit me at once. It was like imposter syndrome, that feeling that I didn't deserve her, or that I wasn't good enough for her. Was I just a roll in the hay, like another notch in her lipstick case?

"What's wrong?" Maria's voice ripped through my thoughts like a machete. "You froze on me."

"Sorry, I'm freaking out a little bit." One of my arms covered my breasts, while the other snaked down to conceal my crotch.

"Don't be afraid of me, Caroline," Maria gazed down at my face. "I want you. No, I need you. Since I moved to North

Carolina you've been my one constant, the woman I rely on the most."

"I am your assistant, so perhaps you're…"

"No," Maria frowned. "You don't understand how difficult it was for me to accept my feelings for you. There's a boundary we shouldn't have crossed, but I couldn't help the way I feel about you." Maria leaned down and kissed the tip of my nose. "I, well, I really feel something for you. Without you, I'd be so lost."

I couldn't believe my ears.

"If you think we're moving too fast, we can stop right now, Caroline." Maria brushed her lips over mine. "But you should know that I want to make love to you more than anything else in the world. I don't know what you've done to my heart." Her voice deepened with every syllable, then she stared at me for a long moment.

"Okay," I whispered.

"Okay what?" Maria lifted a brow.

"Please, make love to me." My heart galloped in my chest.

A slow smile spread across Maria's cheeks, then she moved down my trembling body until her face hovered over my pussy. She licked up my folds, and when I felt her tongue on my clit I groaned. Maria slipped a finger inside me, and electricity zipped through my limbs. My eyes snapped shut as pleasure shot through my core. It had been so long since I'd felt wanted by anyone, much less an opera diva who made love like a Goddess.

Maria's mouth and fingers worked in tandem, not giving me the chance to say no, or to hesitate. But now that I was so close, so damned close to coming it would be impossible for me to utter a word. My legs and arms quivered and I gripped the sheets with both hands. A whining noise came from my chest, and I felt Maria's lips lock around my clit. Without thinking my hands gripped the sides of Maria's head, holding her in place.

"Oh God, I'm coming!"

Maria kept going, her lips, tongue, and fingers working in tandem while my body thrashed beneath her. I sobbed as my orgasm took control of my body, and after what seemed like forever Maria folded her body into mine like the perfect spoon.

"Thank you," I sighed, and realized tears were streaming down my cheeks. "This was perfect."

"No," Maria whispered in my ear. "You are perfect."

———

I'd woken up with my head on Maria's chest, which gently moved up and down with only the occasional sigh. A feeling of serenity filled me, so unlike my usual state of being. It was like the most exquisite drug I could imagine, and I knew if this, whatever this was that Maria and I shared was to end, I'd probably end up in rehab to kick the habit. I couldn't believe I was in her bed, my arm draped casually over her taut stomach and one leg wrapped over thigh. It would have been easy to stay like that, but a glance at the clock on the nightstand told me we'd overslept. I brushed my lips over her smooth cheek and disentangled my limbs from hers.

"Where are you going?" Maria mumbled, then pulled me back into her embrace and held me tight. "You can't leave."

A feeling of warmth rushed through me, and I wondered if we had time for a replay of last night. I slid my leg over Maria's crotch and she tightened her grip on me.

"Keep doing that and you will never leave my bed again."

I nuzzled her neck.

"Damn it." Maria muttered, then seconds later she was on

top of me, her face hovering over mine. "I need you. If I don't..."

My phone vibrated on the nightstand, and we both groaned at the same time. Maria snatched it up and drew her arm back as if she was about to pitch it against the wall.

"Don't!" I grabbed it from her, and was disappointed to see a text from Bella.

Picking both of you up at 1

"We'd better get ready. Bella is picking us up in a couple of hours, and that means I have to go home first."

"Just wear something of mine. Surely there is..." Maria began, but I interrupted.

"Coffee. You're out, and unlike superhuman singers, herbal tea won't cut it. I need a caffeine fix. Plus, you're taller and thinner than me. Your clothes won't fit." I pulled Maria down and pecked her on the cheek. I wasn't about to scare her away with morning breath.

Maria leaned her forehead against mine and sighed. "Go now, or you're not leaving my bed."

———

I heard tires squealing outside, and then my phone pinged. It was Bella letting me know she was waiting out front, so I grabbed my bag and headed out.

When I opened the door to my building I froze. Bella's steel gray Jaguar idled in front of the building, with one tire resting on the sidewalk. Maria was in the passenger seat, staring straight ahead, unmoving. I lived on a one-way street, and Bella's car was facing in the wrong direction.

"We have to hurry. I thought you'd both be at Maria's, and I don't want to keep Greta waiting." Bella muttered, and before I'd completely shut the back door, she pressed down on the accelerator and took off. A beat-up Volkswagen hippy-van turned onto the street at the corner and Bella slammed on the brakes, throwing me against the front seat where Maria sat, and then back.

"Oh my fucking GOD!" I shouted, and grabbed my chest. Bella put the Jag in reverse and backed up to the alley and allowed the VW to pass.

"Damn it." Bella said. "We're going to be late, I just know it."

I sat back in the seat and fumbled with the seat belt, and after three attempts finally got it fastened. Maria turned her head toward me, her eyes like saucers and mouthed, "We're going to die."

I opened my mouth to respond, but caught Bella glancing in the rearview mirror and shut my eyes instead. If we were going to die, I didn't want to see it coming. It struck me that I'd only had one opportunity to sleep with Maria in my arms, so I decided to focus on that memory to distract myself from the potential carnage.

"Mamma Mia let me go!"

Bohemian Rhapsody blared from the speakers, and my heart lurched in my chest. Eyes snapping open, I saw Bella run the light on Peace Street, narrowly missing a city bus. Maria reached forward and fumbled with the buttons on the radio until she found the volume and turned it down.

"You don't like Queen?" Bella asked. "I thought everyone did."

"I um, don't want…" Maria started.

"We're thinking of doing a Pops series, kind of like the Boston Pops, and this would be a tremendous song to perform. But the board of directors keeps turning the project down. They say we don't have the budget for it, thanks to you." Bella said, then laughed and patted Maria on the knee, her eyes not on the road. "But, so far you're worth every penny."

"Bella." I said, noticing the light at the corner of Capital Boulevard and Millbrook Rd was fast approaching, and very red. "There's a red..."

"For God's sake, Bella!" Maria shouted. Bella turned her head back toward the road and slammed on the brakes. "You're the worst driver I've ever seen!"

"What can I say?" Bella shrugged her shoulders and cackled. "It's one of my many talents."

———

"You're a gifted performer, Ms. Wagner. If you don't mind, I want to ask you about the loss of your voice, and your struggle to come back to the opera stage."

Greta Dollitz was a tiny bird-like woman who spoke slowly and deliberately, with a touch of a German accent. While she and Maria set up the ground rules for the interview, I snapped pictures of the two of them for social media. Bella sat in the control booth with the engineer. Maria had initially been reluctant to discuss anything besides the current production of Cosi Fan Tutte, not wanting to discuss her personal life. Bella had left the control booth to talk to her, reminding Maria that her personal journey back to the stage would be fascinating for the listeners.

"It's one of the toughest things to happen to a singer, losing your voice on stage in front of thousands of people." Maria said, her voice trembling. She'd never spoken at length with me about this experience and I was as curious as her interviewer.

"Over the last ten years, four major stars have had similar experiences. Montserrat Villazon, Aleksanders Antonenko, Roberto Alagna, and yourself. The difference between you and them is that instead of having surgery on your vocal cords, you opted for a different approach. You went to a controversial singing school in Naples, Italy."

"Elise, my vocal coach, had to teach me to sing all over again, and it was a struggle to say the least." Maria said, shutting her eyes for a brief moment. "She said I'd been taught to sing incorrectly. That almost every singer performing today is being taught the wrong way to sing."

"You studied at The Curtis Institute, one of the premier music schools in the world. So did your conductor, Bella Lombardi. Are you saying that The Curtis Institute is at fault?" Greta took off her wire-frame glasses and peered at Maria in disbelief. I glanced over to the control booth. Bella was frowning.

"No, I do not fault my instructors." Maria said, her brow furrowed. "They teach what they've been taught, which is essentially to sing as loud as you can."

"But, if you're to fill an auditorium and sing over an orchestra, you do have to sing loudly." Greta scribbled something in her notebook and waited for Maria to reply. She took a moment before speaking.

"There's a huge difference between singing with volume and screaming. Elina taught me to sing from the diaphragm, to use my voice differently than I'd originally been taught. Essentially, she taught me to sing using the same techniques used prior to the twentieth century. I'm not a vocal coach, so I'm having a hard time putting this in layman's terms." Maria gave a tight smile, then continued. "Elise's technique works for me, and my instrument has never been in better shape. I cannot speak for other musicians or teachers."

Maria's eyes locked on mine, wordlessly communicating her discomfort. Automatically, I began to stretch my hand out for her to take, but then remembered where I was and withdrew it.

I glanced up to see Greta's eyes trained on me. Blushing, I looked toward the control booth and saw that Bella had her arms crossed over her chest, scowling.

"How did you feel after losing your voice, Maria? Did you ever consider calling it quits?"

"I was devastated, naturally. It was as if someone had ripped my soul out of my body. Music is everything to me. There's no way I can quit. If my training with Elina hadn't worked out, I would have gone under the knife to get my voice back. Getting back on stage was my entire focus." Maria's voice lowered to a whisper.

"Your performance last night was brilliant, and everyone is thrilled you're able to sing onstage again. Your performance as Despina is both comic and poignant. Acting doesn't come easy to many singers, but you had me enthralled from the moment you hit the stage." Greta pivoted gracefully from the more controversial part of the interview. "Tell me, Maria, do you share your character's belief that relationships are a fickle business, and that anyone can be tempted to stray from their lover?"

Maria flushed, then reached across the table and took my hand, an unabashed smile spreading across her cheeks. Her dark eyes glittered in my direction, and I bit my lower lip.

"No. Definitely not."

CHAPTER

Twenty

CAROLINE

AFTER THE INTERVIEW, we went straight to the theater. Maria insisted on driving. Bella must have been used to it, because she handed over her keys with only a half-smile and a lifted eyebrow.

Since the performance wasn't for a few more hours, I showed Maria my broom closet office, gathered up my laptop and then we went downstairs to Rehearsal Room D. Maria had never shown much interest in her social media accounts and I thought she should become more involved. It wouldn't take much effort to boost her followers. All she had to do was post a picture of herself in a short tight dress occasionally.

"I understand why this is important, Caroline. But, I honestly can't think of one single thing about myself that would interest anyone. You know what my life is about. I wake up, rehearse, and perform." Maria grasped my hand in hers and brought it to her lips. "And I take indecent liberties with my assistant."

"Nothing indecent about it." I murmured, then leaned over

and brushed my lips against her cheek. "Now, what are we going to do about the interview?"

"What do you mean? It's already done."

"No, you have to publicize it." I pulled my phone out of my pocket and found Greta's number. I tapped out a quick message for her to contact me with the date and time when the interview was to be aired. "As soon as Greta lets me know when the show airs, I can bombard Facebook and Twitter with announcements. This generates excitement for the fans, plus if the interview gets excellent ratings there's a chance of more interviews taking place in the future."

Maria sighed. "I hate doing interviews. I'd rather kiss you instead."

"I'm not stopping you."

Maria placed her hands on my cheeks, and then the door to the rehearsal room flew open. We jumped apart, as if we were two schoolgirls being caught by their Sunday School teacher.

"I don't give a…" Charlie, the makeup artist, stopped speaking as soon as he noticed us. The stage director, Peter, was behind him, a look of frustration evident on his face.

"Did you two need the room? Because we can take care of this stuff somewhere else." I grabbed my leather bag, dumped my phone in it and stood. Maria stayed seated, entranced by the potential drama brewing in front of us. Charlie scowled, then elbowed his way past Peter and raced out of the room.

"Sorry you had to see that." Peter took off his glasses and wiped them on his shirt. "Just a personnel issue." He put his glasses back on and sighed. "Professionalism isn't Charlie's strong suit." Then he spun around and left. Maria giggled, grabbed my hand and pulled me down onto her lap. I ran my fingers through her chestnut hair, relishing the softness, and that always-present lavender scent.

"You see? Compared to everyone else, my life is much too dull for social media."

———

Maria's rich, powerful voice filled the theater, and as usual I stood in the wings mesmerized by her. The other singers were talented, but Maria had something different. Even if I could divorce my personal feelings from this observation, I knéw Maria had that elusive star-quality most performers could only dream of. Then it struck me that if I could see it, so could everyone else.

"You won't be in North Carolina for long. And what will happen to me when you're tempted away by more money and fame?" I whispered, then heard more whispering behind me. Turning my head, I saw Peter and Charlie, and neither looked happy. Peter gestured toward a face chart he had in his hand, then placed his index finger over his lips. Instead of quieting down, Charlie yanked the chart out of his hand, tore it in two, then stomped off.

"Shit." I heard him mutter, then his gaze landed on me and his eyes lit up. Peter hurried over, and I noticed beads of sweat on his upper lip.

"I need you to take over for Charlie. He was going to touch up the chorus members, plus he was handling the character of Dorabella. This is the face chart for her." He handed me the ripped up paper. "I'll get someone to help with Maria's costume changes."

Fear gripped me. I didn't know how Maria would react, plus I'd not studied the other cast members makeup charts. Peter took me by the elbows.

"Look, just wing it for Christ's sake. Go!"

———

I dipped a latex sponge in a jar of cold cream, then began removing Maria's makeup. "Maria, you've been in countless productions. It doesn't matter whether I'm assisting you or if someone else is. We're all professionals here…"

"… then I took the towel from her shaking hands and mopped up my own sweat. God, it was mortifying." Maria plopped back in the director's chair and shook her head. "*You* are my assistant. I can't bear it when other people touch me." Maria shut her eyes automatically when I held up a cotton square. I held it against her eye for a moment before wiping away the thick eyeliner. "So what happened to the makeup artist Charlie?"

"Beats me. I'm sure I will find out soon enough."

Honestly, I didn't care. I was still smarting from not getting the makeup artist job. Then a feeling of gratitude washed over me. If I'd gotten that position, would Maria and I have become involved? Plus, was Peter a nightmare to work for? Would I have hated the job?

"You've got an intense look on your face, Caroline. Are you all right?" Maria took my hand and brought it to her lips.

"I'm fine. Well, I'm just feeling tired. I had to touch up most of the chorus, and Dorabella's makeup was piled on an inch thick. She had a ten-minute break in Act two, so I wiped some of it off and re-did it. She hugged me, which was nice. Maybe that was the problem with Charlie?" I shrugged my shoulders, then turned toward the makeup counter to clean my brushes. Seconds later Maria's palm was squeezing my ass.

"Her makeup looked awful. I noticed that during prepro-duction. All of the female characters look like hookers." Maria laughed. "I lucked out with you. I'll tell you one thing, though.

They'd better have a replacement for Charlie soon, because I won't stand for it if they take you away from me again."

———

Maria's car passed my street. She hadn't said that she wanted me to sleep over, and though I wanted to be with her, it kind of bothered me she just assumed I would.

A minute later Maria pulled into the parking lot of her building and switched off the ignition. Then she got out of the car and bounded toward the front entrance, not looking once to see if I was behind her. I grabbed my leather bag out of the back seat and got out of the car, inwardly debating whether I should just follow along behind her or walk the two blocks to my place.

Maria punched in the code for the door and opened it, and then she turned around and cocked her head. "Aren't you coming inside?"

I kicked at the pavement with my sneaker. "Well, we hadn't discussed it. Do you want me to go to your place?" Of course, I knew she did, but I wanted to hear her say it. Better yet, I wanted her to ask instead of assuming I would do whatever she wanted.

Maria let the front door to the building swing shut and sauntered over to me, placing her hands on my shoulders. "Where else would you go? Do you not want to spend the night? I should've asked, but I just thought it was…"

"Maria," I interrupted. "I want to be with you, but if we're to make this work, I think we need to negotiate a few things first."

"Like what?" Maria's voice dropped an octave.

"Are we still at work? Because even though I'm your personal assistant, that doesn't mean you should assume I'll be at your beck and call twenty- four hours a day. You need to ask me if I want to spend the night, otherwise it feels like an order from my boss. And that's not a very romantic way to start our evening."

"Oh. I'm sorry, Caroline. I guess... "Maria grinned, then placed her hands around the back of my neck. "Caroline, will you please spend the night in my arms? Because I need you there, and can't imagine you sleeping anywhere else." She kissed the tip of my nose, and my knees felt weak.

"Yes, I'd love to spend the night with you."

"Last night wasn't enough, huh?" Maria's black eyes bored into mine while her hand cupped my breast.

"It's never enough." I whispered. Barely a word had been spoken last night. Maria had led me to the bedroom and taken my clothes off. Then she'd made love to me, with an air of possessiveness I'd never experienced with any woman before. Underneath the domineering surface, I'd felt something else, a fragility she desperately sought to hide.

"It's only nine. We have time to..."

My phone pinged on the nightstand.

"Fuck." Maria growled and rolled off me. "I hate your phone."

"You're not the only one." I sighed, then sat up against the headboard and grabbed it. It was a message from Angela. "Damn it."

> Please be at Bella's office by 11 for a meeting- alone

CHAPTER
Twenty~One
CAROLINE

"YOU CAN GO IN NOW, CAROLINE,"

I nodded toward the receptionist and stood, my knees wobbling. I'd been waiting for ten minutes, though I'd arrived for the meeting on time. Whatever it was Bella and Angela wanted to talk to me about, it couldn't be good.

I told Maria about the meeting, but not the part about me attending it alone. When she got out of bed to get showered and changed, I told her it was most likely about tedious paperwork, or publicity stuff. She'd hopped back in bed, rolled over and fell back to sleep.

Hesitating a moment before knocking, I willed the butterflies in my stomach to behave. Then I took a deep breath and softly rapped on the door.

"Good morning, Caroline." Bella said as she opened the door, then she gestured toward the table in the center of the room. "Have a seat."

Angela was wearing a simple navy sheath, with her usual strand of pearls around her neck. She nodded her head as I sat.

Peter's face was unreadable, but as soon as I sat, he took off his glasses and wiped them on his sleeve. His eyes were bloodshot, and purple shadows indicated a sleepless night.

"Coffee?" Bella gestured toward the carafe and cups at the center of the table. I poured myself a cup, careful not to spill it since my hands were trembling. Out of the three of them, Bella appeared the calmest, a *Mona Lisa* smile resting on her face the entire time.

"Well, let's get to business." Angela said, but before she could say anything else I cleared my throat and spoke.

"Why isn't Maria here? Shouldn't she know about... whatever this is?"

Angela shifted in her seat, then took a sip of coffee, leaving a slight imprint of her mauve lipstick on the rim. "This meeting is about *your* future with the Opera, Caroline."

The butterflies in my stomach went wild. Had Angela discovered that I was involved with Maria? "Am I in trouble for something?"

Bella chuckled, then patted me on the arm. "No. You've done nothing wrong."

"That bastard Charlie..." Peter growled, then Angela cut him off.

"Peter. Let's keep this professional. It's against policy to talk about a former employee and their reasons for being terminated." She turned her head in my direction. "Caroline, Charlie is no longer with us."

That was corporate language that meant Charlie had been fired. But, whenever I heard, "So and so is no longer with us," the first thing that came to mind was that the person was dead.

"Fine. But, I want Caroline to know that the behavior Charlie displayed will not be tolerated." Peter's voice shook, and his face was beet red.

"Why do I need to know about Charlie's behavior?" I asked, then took a small sip of my coffee. Angela reached over and patted Peter's shoulder. Then she sighed and answered my question.

"We want to offer you the position of Makeup Designer for the Opera. Your performance has been exceptional, and we know that you would be just as professional in the makeup designer position as you have been as Maria's assistant. You would report directly to Peter."

The coffee went down the wrong pipe, and I coughed. Bella pounded me lightly on the back until the coughing fit subsided.

Professional? She definitely doesn't know about me and Maria.

"Angela, Caroline will hear about why Charlie was terminated, eventually. Don't you think it best if she hears it from us?" Bella drummed her fingers on the table and rolled her eyes. Angela cleared her throat and shot Bella her an annoyed look.

"Bella, you know it's against policy to speak about..." She began, and then Peter interrupted her.

"First, Charlie was unable to work well with others, namely me. He couldn't accept criticism, plus his work was erratic. Some days he was on top of things, and other days his work was heavy-handed and sloppy. Then, to make matters worse, the psycho called me at two in the morning, drunk. My wife answered my phone thinking it was an emergency. The language Charlie used was... extremely inappropriate." Peter shook his head. "I should've gone with my gut instincts and hired you in the first place, Caroline. But Bella and Angela insisted that..."

"Peter, that's enough." Angela smacked the table.

It suddenly dawned on me that I was originally supposed to have been the makeup designer. But Bella and Angela had decided against it. I glanced over at Angela, who looked down at the open file in front of her, a hint of color staining her pale cheeks.

Bella poured himself a cup of coffee, then grinned at me sheepishly. "What can I say? I knew you and Maria would hit it off, though I had no idea just how well you girls would get along."

Angela's eyes narrowed, and she tilted her head to the side.

"So, how do you think she will take it?" Bella asked me. I glanced over toward Angela, who appeared very confused. She swiveled her head back and forth between Bella and me.

"What's the big deal about Maria? We'll have another PA for her within days." Angela shrugged, then tugged on her left pearl earring.

My cheeks burned. I knew she'd figure it out eventually, but considering she was offering me the job I'd always wanted, I figured that pissing her off right now was the last thing I should do.

Bella turned to me and grinned. "It's not that big a deal, Caroline. She didn't fire Lilith when she found out about us."

Angela's nostrils flared. "Wait, a minute. You mean to tell me you've been fuc... having an affair with my star singer?!"

I flinched.

"For crying out loud Angela, what's the problem? Two people meet, fall in love..." Bella began. But then the office door flew open. Maria stood in the doorway, glaring, while the receptionist kept trying to peek over her shoulders.

"This sweet woman tried to keep me out of your office That set off numerous alarm bells, so I decided to let myself in." Maria lifted her chin and smiled, shut the door, then crossed the room and stood behind my chair, squeezing my tense shoulders.

Maria was in full diva mode, and it was both terrifying and erotic.

"Before you fill me in on the details of this meeting, let me make one thing perfectly clear." Maria's voice dropped to a whisper..

"If anything happens to Caroline, I'm history."

CHAPTER

Twenty~Two

MARIA

"WELL. Isn't anyone going to speak?"

I moved from behind Caroline and paced around the room, waiting for answers. When I'd first walked in, the first thing I noticed was all the color draining from Caroline's face. That was clue number one that my suspicions were correct.

They wanted to split us up.

"Maria, I think you are overreacting." Angela tapped her pen against the open file in front of her.

"Caroline gets called to a meeting without me. Since she is my personal assistant, I find that alarming. In my mind, you are keeping something from me, or trying to drive a wedge in between us somehow." My knuckles cracked from clenching my fists, sharp staccato sounds that echoed in the tense air.

"Perhaps this has absolutely nothing to do with you? Have you ever thought about that?" Peter muttered darkly, then he winced. "Ow!"

Angela, who was sitting next to Peter, must have kicked him. At least one of them knew enough not to treat the star of their opera company like shit. The stage director put his face in his hands and sighed.

"Maria, please sit down and we will tell you what our meeting with Caroline was about." Angela sighed, then poured herself a cup of coffee. There wasn't another chair at the table, so I perched against the edge of Bella's desk and folded my arms over my chest.

"The reason we didn't invite you to this meeting is because it involves a personnel matter. According to our policy, we conduct these meetings in private." Angela glared daggers in Bella's direction. "Not that everyone here gives a fu… cares about following procedure."

I'd never seen this chilly woman skirt the borders of unprofessionalism before. It was rather amusing.

Bella couldn't wipe the smirk off of her face. She looked like she was enjoying Angela's minor meltdown.

I was behind Caroline, so I couldn't see her face. Her shoulders were stiff, and I wanted nothing more than to scoop her up in my arms and comfort her. She didn't seem to understand that I held all the cards in this meeting. There was no way in hell they would risk losing me by splitting us apart.

"Why did you hire me for the PA position?" Caroline's voice quavered.

Angela opened her mouth to speak, but Bella cut her off.

"Eye candy. We wanted more than anything to keep our star singer happy." Bella glanced up and caught my eye. "Caroline, if you haven't looked in the mirror lately, you are a beautiful woman. I went to school with Maria, and I knew what types of girls she went out with. You were the perfect…"

"Oh my fucking GOD!" Angela's pen flew out of her hand. "Bella, you insisted that Caroline was the best candidate for the PA position because she was cool-headed, and wouldn't lose her temper with that prima donna." She pointed her finger at me. "Now I hear the truth. You were pimping Caroline out!"

"Prima donna?!" I yelled, and Bella snapped, "I was not!"

"This is a fucking lawsuit waiting to happen." Angela muttered, then pointed at Caroline. "I wouldn't blame you in the slightest for filing a sexual harassment claim against us. Jesus, all I wanted to do was make you the damned makeup designer, and now I learn you were..."

"Angela, maybe it's best for you to stop now." Peter shifted his bloodshot eyes in Caroline's direction. "All you're doing is giving her ideas. And Bella, what the hell were you thinking?"

Silence settled over the room, only broken by the sound of Angela's fingernails drumming on the table. I reached out and laid my hands on Caroline's shoulders.

"Well, now," Angela steepled her fingers under her chin, "So you two are an item. What's done is done. Marvelous work, Bella." She rolled her eyes and stared at Caroline. "Have you ever thought it might be better for the two of you to not work in such close proximity? I mean, the makeup designer position would give you both a little space, but you'd still be working together."

So, they must have fired the crazy makeup artist. Now they wanted Caroline for the job. It was just as I suspected. This woman wanted to tear us apart.

"Absolutely not." I stood. "Caroline belongs by my side."

"Why don't we ask Caroline what she thinks." Bella leaned back in his chair and grinned. "We're all discussing her fate without even asking her what she wants to do."

I walked around the table so I could see Caroline's expression. Her chin trembled, and her skin was drained of color. I felt my heart race when I noticed that she wouldn't meet my gaze. Finally, she spoke in a strained voice.

"May I speak to Maria alone?"

CHAPTER
Twenty-Three
CAROLINE

MARIA SAT at the piano in Rehearsal Room D. Her shoulders slumped forward, brown eyes trained on her lap.

When I asked to be alone with Maria, Bella had immediately piped up that it was an excellent idea, and ushered us to the empty rehearsal room. As soon as the door shut behind Bella, Maria seated herself at the piano and avoided my gaze.

"Are you afraid of me?" Maria murmured, not looking in my direction. "Because when you asked for us to be alone, it was fear I saw in your eyes. I don't want you to feel scared."

I sat on the metal chair next to the grand piano and sighed. "Maria, I'm not afraid of you. Never think I am. What terrifies me is…" I scrambled to come up with the right words, "…not having control over my life."

Maria's hands crashed down on the keys, playing an angry chord. "Everything was fine until that woman decided to take you away from me." She stood and paced about the room. "I don't think you understand how frightened I am of losing you, Caroline. I've never felt this way about anyone before. That night on stage at the Royal Opera House when I lost my voice, I felt helpless. It's not an emotion I have an awful lot of experience with, and right now, I'm feeling that exact way." She stopped in her tracks and focused her gaze on mine. Then she turned around, and I noticed a subtle trembling in her shoulders.

"Maria, nobody is taking me away from you." I crossed over to where she was and wrapped my arms around her from behind. "I'm not going anywhere. But I..."

She spun around and pulled me into her chest. "Caroline, unlike what happened with the loss of my voice, I now have some control. They dare not cross me, unless they want me gone from the opera."

I pushed against her and held Maria at arm's length. In her eyes I saw a fiery determination, laced with insecurity and sadness. Almost like the lonely girl I'd sensed inside of Maria that Saturday afternoon watching Moonstruck, shoulder to shoulder. Her instincts were spot on, though. But it wasn't Maria I feared. It was the decisions I had to make, and the impact they would have on both of us.

If there *was* a both of us when I finished saying what needed to be said.

"Maria, I need space to think about..."

"Angela is driving you away from me." Maria stepped back and opened her mouth to speak again, but I interrupted.

"The makeup designer position is the one I originally applied for. Then Bella intervened, and she made me your assistant." My voice had risen, and I fought to keep it down.

"Thank God." Maria grinned. "Bella is more than a decent conductor. She's an excellent matchmaker, too." Maria moved forward with open arms, but instead of embracing her, I stepped back and rubbed my forehead. Then I straightened my spine and locked eyes with her.

"I want the job, Maria."

She froze, her arched eyebrows shooting toward the ceiling.

"I got my degree in theatrical makeup. It's what I always wanted to…"

"So, you got the job you always wanted. Now you're dumping me." Maria whispered. Her innate energy, usually piercing, and so damned bright, had dimmed. For a moment I believed it was my fault, that I'd let her down. I wanted to rush into her arms and tell her I would turn the job down, but I knew if I did, I could never forgive myself.

"Maria," I stammered, "I don't know where you got that idea from, but I'm exhausted, and I need time to organize my thoughts. Everything has happened so suddenly. In a matter of days we've gone from boss and employee to… I'm not sure *what* it is we share. Are we lovers, girlfriends?" I sighed, then forced myself to continue. "I'm offered the job of my dreams, makeup designer for a major opera company. Now you insist that I'm leaving you, because I don't want to be your personal assistant, *or* your lover." I grabbed my leather bag off the chair and draped the strap over my shoulder.

"Wait, I'm…" Maria began, but I held up my hand, walked to the door and opened it.

"Maria, other people have controlled me for too long. I'm taking the job, even if it means losing you."

She moved forward, and my heart melted when I saw a tear snaking down the side of her nose. But instead of giving in to the siren call of her arms, I walked through the door and forced myself not to look back.

————

"A shot of tequila and a beer, please."

"I'll have the same." A woman's voice drawled from behind me. I turned to see who it was, and inwardly groaned when I saw it was Loretta Anne, the eccentric cellist from the symphony. I glanced down at my watch, wondering why she was here. This was usually the time the symphony rehearsed. She wore all black, including the chopsticks holding her pink hair in place. She was like a southern Mrs. Slocombe from that British TV show, Are You Being Served.

"May I join you, sugar?"

I nodded, and she sat on the stool next to me. The bartender, whose name I think was Blaise, sat our drinks in front of us and waggled his eyebrows. He was wearing a black leather baseball hat and hadn't stopped smiling since I'd walked in.

"You two look like you need it. Surprised to see ya'll so early in the day though." He turned and grabbed a tray of glasses from the side of the bar and began putting them away. Loretta Anne and I were the only people in the bar, and when I glanced down at my phone, I saw why. It was only two in the afternoon.

"Dollface, you look like someone kicked your puppy." Loretta Anne raised her glass. "I'm sure I look the same, so I'm in good company." I clinked my shot glass against hers and threw back the foul-tasting tequila. Normally the woman made me nervous. She usually was all hands and double entendres, but oddly enough I was almost grateful for her company.

"So, what are you doing here so early in the day?" I stared straight ahead at the mirror behind the bar. Loretta Anne bit into a wedge of lime, shuddered, then spoke to my reflection.

"On this day thirty-one years ago, I vowed to love honor and cherish a Mr. William Thorne Vanderbilt Floyd. Everyone called him Vandy. He was quite a catch. Tall, blond hair and green eyes, and muscles you could only get from hard work. And on this same day, seven years later, he left me." She looked down at her lap, then glanced up and caught my eye in the mirror. They shimmered, a veil of dampness threatening to spill down her cheeks.

"Oh, I'm so sorry." I murmured, embarrassed to feel so... lost. Lost over a woman I'd only had for a few days. What she must be going through was far worse than my problems with Maria.

"It's water under the bridge, sweet pea. Water under the bridge. But, I still miss him. So every year I take this day off to celebrate the time we had together." Loretta Anne snapped her fingers and the bartender glanced up, a look of irritation crossing his face. "Another round of shots for me and this young lady, please."

While the bartender poured the drinks I tried to think of something to say, to make the woman feel better. Jesus, the man up and left her on their anniversary. I couldn't imagine how that would make me feel.

"I don't know you well, Loretta Anne, but nobody deserves to be dumped on their anniversary. That takes a special kind of..."

Loretta Anne laid her hand on my arm, threw her head back and laughed. "Oh, bless your heart. He didn't dump me, sugar. No man would *ever* leave me that way. Vandy is in a better place now. Cancer."

My mouth dropped open, and my cheeks burned. Now I really felt like an idiot.

"Darling, it's okay. I've had many years to mourn. Though I think of him often, I learned that life is too short to wallow. So, I allow myself one day every year to celebrate the time we had together." She stopped talking when the bartender set the drinks in front of us. We both picked up the shots and instead of speaking to my reflection in the mirror, she turned toward me and spoke.

"To love. It's the only thing worth living for, and you never know how long you will have it." She placed an arm around my back and downed her drink with her other hand. I placed my drink on the bar, untouched.

"So, why aren't you looking after the star of the opera today?"

I opened my mouth to speak, but nothing came out. My problems seemed so petty and small compared to hers.

"Cat got your tongue?" She removed her arm from behind me and started digging in her purse, fishing a rhinestone compact out of her bag. She flipped it open and examined her face, then patted powder on her forehead.

"I'm, well, it's just after hearing your…"

"Darling, I don't have a problem with Vandy's passing. I just miss him, that's all." She snapped the compact shut and smiled. "I wonder what our life would have been like, oh, and I…"

"I'm taking over as makeup artist for the opera, and Maria's taking it the wrong way." I blurted out. Loretta Anne's eyes widened. "I'm sorry, I shouldn't have interrupted."

"Sweet pea, life is for the living. Now go on, tell Loretta Anne all about it. Oh, and I must know if the rumors are true. Are you two an item?"

"There are rumors about us?" I thought we'd been pretty good at being discreet.

"Hon, all you have to do is look at the two of you together. It's as plain as the nose on your face she's smitten with you. So, let me guess. The prima donna feels threatened, or thinks you're abandoning her, right?"

"It's… complicated."

"Everyone says they want a drama-free love, no tears, pain or work. But, life doesn't work that way. Trust me, I know all about it. Romance is fucked up, but fun." She sipped her beer and sighed. "And God, I miss it. You know, I like to talk shit like any other girl, but there's been no one else in my life since Vandy. No one compares, and, well, I guess if I wanted it bad enough, I wouldn't have stayed single all of these years. Oh, look who's here." Loretta Anne spun around on the stool. Bella's wife Lilith was pushing the door to the bar open. When she saw us she waved and headed in our direction. She pecked Loretta Anne on the cheek before sitting on the other side of her.

"You doing okay, Loretta Anne?" She murmured, her eyes filled with concern.

"Of course I am. I have this lovely young woman to keep me company." She gestured toward me, then asked her a question. "Lilith, why the hell aren't you at rehearsal?"

"Bella canceled it. Said there was some sort of emergency she had to take care of. Oh, and the assistant conductor is on vacation." Lilith glanced in my direction. "I was also told to keep my eye out for you. Apparently, Maria isn't happy at the moment, and you have something to do with it."

I groaned and covered my face with my hands. I sensed that I might be held responsible for Maria's behavior. It pissed me off, because she was a grown woman, and I had no control over her. Or anyone else for that matter. But nobody in this damn town seemed to realize it. I heard the sound of the bar entrance opening, and then I felt a heavy hand on my shoulder and glanced up.

Fuck. Could this day get any worse?

"Hey, you!" Blaise rushed over to where we were sitting. "You're not allowed in here. If you leave now, there won't be any trouble."

Loretta Anne and Lilith stared at us, eyebrows raised.

"It's cool, man. I saw Caroline through the window. I just need to talk to her for a minute." My ex's voice was different somehow, more assured.

Blaise gave me a questioning look. I smiled weakly and shrugged.

"You have to go." The bartender pointed at Marilyn. "If she wants to talk to you, you'll have to leave. Sorry, but rules are rules." Blaise crossed his arms over his chest and glared.

Marilyn's eyes were clear, and she appeared sober, unlike me. I downed the rest of my beer and turned toward her.

"Let me pay my check and we can go somewhere else to talk."

CHAPTER
Twenty-Four

CAROLINE

I TRIPPED TWICE WALKING down Peace Street, and both times Marilyn caught me. My nerves were shot, and the beer and tequila were amplifying the dread I felt. Every few moments I'd sneak a glance in Marilyn's direction. She appeared healthier than I'd seen her in years, her tan skin glowing in the afternoon sun, and his dark glossy curls glistened.

"So, when did you start drinking?" She quietly asked, startling me. I never expected to hear her questioning my drinking habits, though come to think of it, I had been drinking more.

"Well, um, you are kinda catching me at an awful time. A lot going on." I mumbled, then realized we were approaching my street. Marilyn automatically turned toward my apartment, and without thinking I grabbed her elbow.

"No, um, not my place. Let's walk over to the park and sit in the gazebo." I didn't want her in my home. Whenever she crossed over the threshold dreadful things happened, and they usually involved a shedding of clothes. Though I was positive that wouldn't happen, I didn't want to give her the wrong idea.

"Sure." Marilyn gave me a sheepish grin and shrugged. Only a few months ago I would've taken her home, knowing we would end up in bed and hating myself for it once she'd left. Then, I'd wait in vain for her to call or text, and within a few weeks I'd vow to have nothing to do with her again.

When I saw the park come into view, it suddenly struck me that Maria might catch us. Her building was right behind the park, its tall shadow reaching past the gazebo where we were going.

"Hey. Are you still coming?" Marilyn was a few feet in front of me, looking back to where I'd stopped walking. I glanced up to the top of the apartment building, imagining Maria staring down at us from the penthouse balcony. I knew she wouldn't be able to tell who we were from such a significant height, but I was still paranoid.

"Yeah, sorry, just a lot on my mind." I forced my feet to move, and moments later we sat side by side in the gazebo overlooking an azalea garden. We sat in silence for a few moments, and I wondered what the hell Marilyn wanted from me. Unless it was her usual every-six-month tease, I hadn't a clue. Then she leaned her shoulder against mine and tried to take my hand. I scooted a couple of inches away and scowled.

"I guess I deserved that." She muttered, then placed her face in her hands and sighed.

"Yeah, you do." I got to my feet and sat on the bench opposite to her. "What were you expecting? A tumble in the sheets for old time sakes? So you could ignore me for a few months until you..."

"I'm sorry." Marilyn interrupted. "That's why I wanted to speak with you. To make amends for... the shitty way I've treated you. Caroline, you're the kindest woman I've ever known, and I took advantage of you whenever I got the chance."

Her words were unexpected, jarring. Marilyn's brown eyes met mine, and I noticed a flush creeping up her neck.

"But, I didn't come here to get you in bed again. It's just… I don't know… the memory of you. When I see you up close, all the good times come flooding back, and I want them again. You have this power over me, Caroline. Sincerely, I wasn't trying to take advantage of you."

I let her words wash through me. Being Marilyn's easy lay had become a habit for me too. But, I wouldn't go through another few months of guilt and bitterness just to feel her arms around me again. Then it dawned on me: I didn't want her anymore. I eyed her as she waited for me to reply, noting her hesitation and fear. If she wasn't here for a sentimental roll in the hay for old time's sake, what did she want?

"Why now?" I asked. "What happened? Do you need money? A place to live? Because I can't do…"

"No." Marilyn stood and turned away. "I don't want anything from you. Just a little time to say what I need to say."

Minutes passed, and neither of us spoke. Marilyn stared straight ahead, not meeting my gaze. I glanced down at my phone, hoping Maria had sent me a text, and dreading it too. There wasn't a message, and I stuffed the phone in my bag and prayed that Marilyn would just get this over with. As curious as I was to know why she was here, I had more important things I wanted to deal with.

"I quit drinking." She murmured.

"Again?" I snorted, and instantly regretted it. No matter how I felt about her now, Marilyn's sobriety was important.

"Fuck you." Marilyn pressed her lips together. "Sorry. I know I deserve that. But, seriously, I can't drink anymore."

"Why did you stop?" I asked, then felt a pang of queasiness. If she said it was because of me, I would scream. She'd said that to me before, and it had never stopped her from picking the bottle up again.

"Shit, I was hoping you wouldn't ask that." Marilyn sighed, and sat down next to me. She stared up at the ceiling of the gazebo. "Two weeks ago I began feeling funny. Nauseous, light-headed and my stomach hurt. I went to the doctor, and she noticed my blood pressure was really high, so he checked me into the hospital."

Marilyn had always had issues with her blood pressure, and I'd told her on more than one occasion that drinking made it worse.

"They ran tests, and it turned out that I had pancreatitis, and it was because of my drinking. The doctor said if I didn't stop it would only get worse, that I could…" Her words trailed off. A little orange rubber ball was wedged under a corner of the wood next to the bench. Marilyn kicked at it until it came loose. It bounced against the bench in front of us and landed next to my shoe. I kicked it out of the gazebo, and it bounced into the azalea's.

"I needed help, so after they released me I went to an AA meeting. They have these steps you're supposed to follow and…"

"I've heard about the steps." I mumbled, wondering if even her brush with death would keep her sober.

"I've only been sober for a few days, and my sponsor told me to take my time working the steps, but when I saw the eighth step, I immediately thought of you." Marilyn turned toward me. "*Make a list of all persons we had harmed and became willing to make amends to them all.* I realized that if I didn't at least try to make amends with you for all the crap I've done that I'd never get better. You moved to Raleigh because of me, and all I did was let you down. Caroline, you deserved so much better than me. I'm truly sorry for any pain I caused you."

"I don't know what to say." Of all the unexpected things this crazy day was throwing in my direction, this was completely out of left-field. Then, my knuckles popped, and I glanced down to see my hands balled into fists. My body tensed, and I felt a searing heat spreading from limb to limb.

"I honestly don't give a fuck." I bit off the words. "You dragged me here to say you're sorry. Well, big fucking deal. The day I met you was the worst day of my life." My voice rose, and I raced out of the gazebo, the sight of Marilyn making my blood boil. I raced toward Maria's apartment building, then felt a pain in my gut and stopped. I hadn't felt so angry before in my life. First, any chance of a relationship with Maria was dwindling by the second. Second, they'd offered me the job of my dreams and I wasn't sure if it was worth losing Maria over. Third, my alcoholic ex just had to choose today of all days to show up. I felt pressure building behind my eyes and then felt a hand on my shoulder. I spun around, prepared to say my worst to Marilyn.

"Hey, I'm sorry." Tears were streaming down her cheeks. "It was selfish of me to lay this all on you now. I should've listened to my sponsor. She said you might react like this and…"

"Have you ever realized that it's not all about you?!" I screamed, and a fleck of spit hit her cheek. "For fuck's sake. I've had it. You dragged me here from Pennsylvania and dumped me. Then I get fired from a job for something I didn't do. To add icing to this layer of hate-cake, I fell in love with my boss who wants me to give up my fucking dream job so we can be together. Have you noticed the thread stringing all this together, Marilyn?" I marched back to the gazebo and snatched my bag off of the bench with trembling hands. Marilyn followed behind me, and I growled at her through clenched teeth. "I have no control over my life. It's like nobody gives a damn what I want. Not Maria, not Montaldo's, and especially not you!"

I glared at her, daring Marilyn to say another word. She could take her far-too-late apologies and stick them up her ass.

Marilyn's gaze softened. A few years ago I would've melted at the sight, but now it only made my pulse thud even harder.

"Are you in love with… Maria? She's your boss, right?"

"What do you care?" I muttered, then without warning a sob tore through my chest. I sank down onto the bench, and a second later Marilyn was next to me. She wrapped her arms around me, and I tried to push her away. But then it was too late, and my anger and frustrations came out in a downpour of tears.

———

"You're lying to yourself."

"What are you talking about?" I wiped at my eyes with the back of my hand.

"You say you have no control over your life. While it's true that there are certain things out of your control, this thing with your boss isn't one of them."

"What are you talking about?" I opened my bag and fished out a pack of tissues.

"Have you told her how you feel? That you love her?" Marilyn's arm was around my shoulder and I leaned back against it.

"No. But Maria must know that I…"

"She's not a mind reader. Tell her how you feel. Take control of the situation by being honest. If she's a narcissist, she'll tell you to not take the job. Then you'll know where she really stands and you can make the decisions you need to make. If she loves you, she'll want your hopes and dreams to come first. All of this is in your control, Caroline. It's up to you." Marilyn removed her arm and stood, then offered her hand to pull me up. When I got to my feet, she gave me a hug and murmured in my ear.

"And if she turns out to be a total asshole, she'll have to answer to me."

CHAPTER
Twenty-Five
CAROLINE

THE PHONE BUZZED on my nightstand, waking me from a chemical sleep. I'd taken three sleeping pills last night, wanting to be knocked out cold. Mostly it worked, aside from dreams I couldn't recall. I sat up and stared at the phone, then noticed the time. It was only 8:30 in the morning. The symphony office was still closed, so it probably was Maria, wanting me to pick up something from the store for her, or... wait. We'd had a fight. The fog in my brain was preventing me from thinking straight. If it was Maria, it wasn't because she'd run out of vegan ice cream.

"Shit!" I grabbed at the phone and knocked it to the floor instead. I reached down for it and tumbled to the floor. When I finally had a firm grip on the phone, I rolled over on to my back and held it in front of my face.

First was a message from Angela.

> 10:00 AM MANDATORY MEETING WITH SERGE PETER AND ME

There was a second message from Bella.

> Be at my office at 10. Her Highness wants to meet with you.

I assumed Bella meant Angela. Since her entire message was in caps, I was guessing she was in a tizzy.

The phone buzzed in my hands, and it dropped onto my chest with a thud. A new message from Maria.

> I missed you last night.

My eyes misted over. The reason I'd taken the pills to help me sleep was telling me she'd missed me. My fingers hovered over the keyboard, itching to text Maria back. Instead, I placed it on the nightstand and got up off the floor and perched on the edge of the bed.

Last night I'd sat in silence, curled up on the couch. I wondered if I was making the right decision to accept the makeup designer position. And, after running all the arguments through my head, I'd made a choice.

For once in my life, I would not chase a woman, giving up on my own dreams and desires. I'd left my home up north to follow Marilyn to a strange town, when I could have followed a much surer career path by moving to Philly or New York City. Holding on to that failed romance had cost me so much emotionally, and it set back my career goals. No more shitty retail jobs, and no more putting my needs second.

As much as I cared for Maria, loved her in fact, I had to put myself first. If she couldn't understand why I needed to follow my own path for once in my life, then it would be over between us.

The door to Bella's office was open when I arrived. I poked my head in, hoping to see a carafe of coffee on the table so I wouldn't have to go to the employee lounge. Bella waved me in, and thankfully she poured me a cup of joe and handed it to me.

Angela's back was to the door, so I couldn't see her expression until I sat down next to Bella. My mouth dropped open at the sight of her, and I mentally kicked myself and shut it. Her normally painted face was bare, and it shocked me to discover that she had been painting on her lips. Normally I could detect that sort of thing by just looking at someone. Without war paint her lips were thin, devoid of color, and pressed firmly together. Purple shadows under her eyes indicated lack of sleep, and she wouldn't meet my gaze.

Bella also looked a little worse for wear, and she was wearing head to toe black. Peter was scowling in Angela's direction. His hair was a mess, and if I wasn't mistaken, he was wearing the same shirt he had on yesterday. Apparently, he'd not caught up on his lost sleep from the night before.

"Thank you for coming in so early." Bella said, stifling a yawn. "I don't know how people function in the morning."

"Welcome to the real world." Angela muttered, then poured herself a cup of coffee. The business side of the Virginia Opera and Richmond Symphony kept banking hours, while the artists and musicians rarely started their day until after twelve.

"Caroline, we're sorry that we have to do this, but we must rescind the job offer we made to you. For now, we think it is in the best interest of the Virginia Opera to keep you on as Maria's personal assistant." Angela stated, her voice strained. Peter scowled, and Angela shot him a withering look.

"Let me blunt with you, Caroline. Maria hasn't returned any of our calls, but from what she indicated in yesterday's meeting, she isn't willing to give you up. I mean, as her PA." Bella shook her head back and forth, then grimaced. "Sorry, Caroline. If we'd known Maria would react this way, we would never have offered you the…"

Their words continued while my brain tried to process this latest setback. If what they were saying was true, Maria was threatening to leave if I didn't remain her assistant. I glanced up to see Peter opening his mouth to speak, so I cut him off before this conversation could go any further.

"Let me talk to Maria." My fist hit the table, causing Angela's coffee to splash out of her cup. Her nose flared, and she reached for a napkin to mop it up. "She must know how important this job is to me. Plus, well, there's something else going on with her." Even though everyone present knew about Maria and me, this didn't seem like the time to delve into personal issues.

"Caroline, if you can talk some sense into the woman, I for one would appreciate it." Peter huffed. "As things stand, we'll have to use you as a fill-in for the makeup-designer position, until we hire someone new. The show must go on, and we don't have anyone else who can do the work on such short notice."

"Peter, we have a file full of freelance makeup artists we can…" Angela began, but Bella cut her off.

"Caroline. Talk to Maria, please. We need her and her voice."

I pushed my chair back, grabbed my bag and raced for the door.

"Caroline!" Bella called out as my hand wrapped around the doorknob. "Remember, we need you too. Be careful."

At first I thought she meant be careful of angering Maria, like she would actually do something physical. Then, when I was halfway down the corridor, it struck me.

Bella meant to be careful with my heart.

———

I jogged toward my neighborhood and was halfway there before I realized I should probably have called an Uber. I'd raced out of the Symphony offices with no other thought than I had to get to Maria. By now it would be ridiculous to call a car for what would only be a five-minute drive. I was in the little park down the street from Maria's building, and I leaned against a tree to catch my breath.

Pulling my phone out of my bag, I looked at the message Maria had sent me earlier this morning. I hadn't replied yet, so I shot her a message.

I'll be there in a few minutes

I pushed myself off the tree and jogged toward her apartment building. Halfway there my phone pinged and I stopped to read the message.

Door's open

"I hope your heart is too." I whispered, then jammed the phone in my bag and hurried forward.

———

True to her word, when the elevator opened on the penthouse floor, the solitary door in the hallway stood ajar. I froze, and a river of dizziness flowed through my limbs. It was the doors to the elevator sliding shut in front of my face that finally propelled me forward.

Once I closed the apartment door, I walked hesitantly into the living room. Maria was standing on the balcony, off to the side next to a potted ficus tree I didn't remember getting for her. She wore a sheer black robe that clung to her curves, and the usual lust I felt for her spiked through me. This might be the last time I would ever get to be alone with Maria, and I needed my brain to function without the distraction of my overeager libido.

"Aren't you going to join me?" Maria said, not turning around. I laid my bag down on the coffee table and strolled forward, all the words I had hastily planned to speak, suddenly gone. When I grasped the balcony railing, I noticed her knuckles were white from gripping it so hard. For a few moments we said nothing. The breeze blew Maria's distinctive scent in my direction and I inhaled, then turned toward her.

"So, are you here to gather your belongings? There were only a few items, a couple of t-shirts, you know…" Maria's voice trailed off, and she had still not looked at me once, her attention on the clouds above us.

"Why are you assuming that I want to end our… relationship?"

"When you didn't call, or message me yesterday, I just assumed you were… Christ, Caroline." Maria turned to face me. "I swear to everything holy, all I want is for you to be happy. I'm sorry, so damned sorry, and I made an ass of myself. It's just, well, I'm scared. I've never had a genuine relationship with another woman before." Her smooth voice shook. Though I found it hard to believe that a woman like her had never been involved with anyone else.

"Seriously?" I lifted an eyebrow.

"Caroline, you don't know much about the opera world, do you?" Maria asked. I shook my head, wondering if it was a world I wanted to know more about. From what I'd seen, it was a cutthroat business that drove everyone involved with it stark-raving mad.

"Except for the two years I spent in Italy getting my voice back, I've spent all of my time on the road. The business arrangement I have with the North Carolina Opera isn't normal for a singer of my stature. Spending years with one opera company is a rarity." Maria's fingers reached for my neck, then drew back. "I would spend two months in one city, then move on to the next. There was no time for me to have a life, much less meet a girl I would fall for."

Every bit of moisture in my mouth disappeared with her words. Was Maria telling me that she'd fallen for me?

"You mean, you've never been with a woman before?" I asked, then realized too late how silly it sounded. I should have had the guts to ask her about the falling for me business. Maria barked out a laugh.

"No, of course I have, and a few men too. But, beyond one or two nights, I've never done much dating. I'll also admit it helps my career to be single, or at least to be perceived that way, so I never pursued anyone. Until you." Maria lifted my hand to her mouth and brushed her lips over it.

Nobody had ever kissed my hand before. Blood raced up my neck, and my heart thumped hard. When I looked down toward the parking lot, that dizziness I felt earlier returned, forcing me to meet her wet gaze.

"When I discovered you'd been offered the makeup-artist job, I couldn't think rationally. All I could imagine was that Angela or Bella was trying to force us apart." Maria let go of my wrist and placed it on my shoulder. "Last night, alone in bed, I realized what a fool I'd been. I know my lack of experience with dating isn't an excuse for my behavior, but I'll do anything to earn your forgiveness, Caroline." She hesitated, then pulled me into her chest, tilted my head down and kissed my hair, then pulled her face back and stared me straight in the eye.

"I love you, Caroline Frank. And I'm terrified that I've lost you, before we even had a chance to see where our future lies."

"I love you too." I blurted out, wishing my words were half as poetic as hers. "But, I have to make something perfectly clear before we take this any further."

Maria's teeth split into a smile, and she nodded for me to continue.

"I'm not abandoning you, but I have to follow my dreams too. The makeup-designer position is my first real break in the industry, and I can't turn it down. For too long I've placed my career aspirations in the backseat, putting the needs of others ahead of mine. I'm taking the job. But I want to be with you too. Can't I have both?" I felt a tear leaking out of my eye and I reached up to swipe it away, but Maria did it for me.

"Yes, oh baby, yes. I'll do anything for you. You can work anywhere you like as long as you are there when my head hits the pillow at night." Maria held me tight, and I felt her chest quake, and a strangled sob escaped from her. A light, euphoric sensation filled me, starting at my feet, and within seconds, had taken over my body. For the first time in my life, I felt wanted, needed in fact, and I never wanted this feeling to disappear.

"I love you, Maria." I breathed into her neck, then I felt her lips against my ear.

"I love you too, Caroline."

Epilogue

MARIA- TWO YEARS LATER

"THANKS FOR COMING, MARIA. SIT."

Bella gestured toward the black leather love seat in front of her desk where Angela was seated. I sat next to her, dreading what was about to take place. Angela turned and gave me a saccharine smile. It was a rainy and dark day, and despite the bright florescent lighting, Bella's office was positively gloomy.

"Your contract is up in a couple of months, and we want to know about your future plans." Bella glanced down at the tablet she had in her lap. "You've over-performed for us, and we are now in the top ten for opera houses in the United States. Plus, we're the only opera company on the list that is turning an actual profit."

"Well, it's not all my doing." I murmured. "I'm the singer, and it takes wonderful musicians, a talented conductor, and a dedicated backstage staff."

"Be that as it may, during your two-year contract you've helped propel us into a new stage of the company's life, one that is envied by others." Bella steepled her fingers under her chin. "But let's get to the point. Once the season is done, you're a free agent. What are you doing next?"

I sat back in the seat and sighed. Bella and Angela stared at me, waiting for an answer. According to my agent, I had over a dozen offers from around the globe to choose from, and all were more lucrative than the offer made by the North Carolina Opera. One in particular appealed to me, but Bella and Angela knew I had ties here, had set up a home with my wife Caroline. Would I prefer to stay in one place, or resume my former globe-trotting lifestyle for a higher payout?

"Working here has been a wonderful experience, and Caroline and I have decided to make Raleigh our home base."

Angela and Bella exchanged glances, and I noticed Angela was suppressing a smile. The woman was the ice-queen of the opera, and I wanted to wipe that smug expression off her face.

"But, I still haven't made up my mind about my plans." I leaned back, knowing I had the upper hand in any negotiations.

Angela's lips pressed together in a flat, red line.

"What does Caroline think about this?" Bella asked. For the first time I noticed a smattering of white strands spreading through her black hair, and wondered if stress was the cause, or simple aging. The woman never stopped working, even in the off-season she was constantly composing new music.

"Caroline's thrilled being the makeup designer here. But, she's also had offers…"

"This is about you, not Caroline." Angela stated, a slight edge in her voice.

"Angela," Bella frowned. "If you don't think this is also about Caroline, you aren't seeing the big picture."

"Sorry." She muttered, then glanced down at her tablet. Angela's finger scrolled down the screen, then she pursed her lips and glanced up at me. "Your agent has informed us you've had other offers. I'll be blunt. We can't afford to pay what most other opera companies can, but we can offer you more creative control, stability, and we're prepared to offer you a percentage of the gross."

My mouth dropped open, so I coughed to cover my surprise. It was virtually unheard of for a singer to have a share of ticket sales, but that still didn't mean it would be the best option for me and Caroline.

"Let me speak with my wife," I sighed. "She has decisions of her own to make too."

"How was rehearsal?" I asked Caroline, who grimaced.

"Fucking Peter is getting on my last good gay nerve." She sighed, referring to the stage director. Though they initially got along, over the last six months they'd begun bickering over creative issues. We were on the balcony of our penthouse eating dinner. The dark skies from earlier had vanished, and the sun was setting in a blaze of purples and reds.

"What now?"

Caroline speared a cherry tomato from her salad and pointed it at me. "My schedule. We're about to enter off-season, and he wants me to work on next season's makeup designs during it, which prevents me from taking other jobs." She popped the tomato into her mouth and glanced toward the downtown skyline. The view from our balcony was guaranteed to calm anyone down, it was so stunning.

"Sorry Peter's being so difficult." I sipped my tea and sighed. "I met with Bella and Angela today. They want to know what I am doing next, since my contract is almost up. This means we have some important decisions to make."

"I love my job, but I'm wondering if I should stay with the opera." Caroline pushed her plate to the side and scratched her neck. "But it's hard to give up the security of a steady check."

"You know you don't need to worry about that." I said, then regretted it. Caroline was very independent, and was determined to pay her own way with everything.

"Maria, while I'm grateful to know I won't be homeless or something if I were to lose my job, I'm not ready to be a sugar baby just yet." She laughed. "Though being kept by you wouldn't be half bad."

"I'm not ready to be your sugar mama just yet, babe." I chuckled. "But, my agent presented me with an offer that's hard to refuse."

"Is it with the North Carolina Opera, or somewhere else?" Caroline's face blanked, becoming almost unreadable. I'd known about the offer for several days now, but had been nervous about sharing it with Caroline. When she got her back up about something, she was nearly impossible to reason with. But we lived a shared life now, and I couldn't leave her in the dark.

"It's in Italy. The Teatro dell'Opera di Roma." I murmured, hoping Caroline wouldn't freak out about it. "For two months next autumn I could play the part of Cio-Cio San in Madame Butterfly."

Caroline's eyes darkened, but she said nothing. After an uncomfortable silence, I told her the most important detail.

"For that two months I'll make more money than I would working an entire season with the North Carolina Opera."

"That sounds wonderful," Caroline sighed. "You can't turn that down, especially when it would give you the opportunity to work elsewhere during the season. I don't know how I'll live without you for such a long stretch of time."

"Who says you would have to live without me?"

Caroline grew still. "My job is here. I can't give up my…"

"How would your resumé look if you worked at The Teatro dell'Opera di Roma?" I bit my lip, hoping she'd say yes, and follow me across the ocean to Italy. "I get to choose my makeup artist. It's only for two months, and then we can decide where to go next. In fact, I'm considering asking Bella if I can still work for the North Carolina Opera, but only for one or two productions a season. That way I can still sing for other companies. Or I can save my voice from oversinging, only working a few months a year but still making substantial money."

Caroline stood. "It's very tempting, Maria, and if I were you I'd pack your bags for Rome. But I need to think about this for a little while." Caroline walked behind my chair and kissed the back of my head.

"As much as I love you, Maria, I'm not sure if this is the right career move for me."

———

Caroline went to bed early, and when I entered the bedroom, it was dark. I stripped my clothes off and climbed into bed next to her.

"Maria." Caroline murmured. "I don't want to hold you back. Please know that."

I turned on my side and draped an arm over her chest. "The thought never crossed my mind." I sighed. "I want what's best for both of us, but I must say that if you're considering leaving the North Carolina Opera, now is the best time. You'll have steady work, even if it's just being my makeup artist."

Caroline gripped my hand, then brought to her lips and kissed it. "I know I'll always have work from you, but I don't want success based on your success."

"But you already have success well beyond my career. You've been the makeup designer for two indie films now, and one of them was a hit. You can work just about anywhere. So why not work for me? At least in the beginning. This is a wonderful chance for you to see the world." I curled into Caroline, covering her legs with mine. "Rome is a stunning city, and I want to share it with you."

"Let's do it." Caroline stated, her voice thick with emotion. "I'm miserable working for Peter, and you're right. A gig in Rome would look excellent on my resumé, plus I'd get to experience the most romantic city in the world with you by my side." She kissed my cheek. "Though I must admit I'll hate giving up our home here. I love this apartment."

I climbed on top of Caroline and kissed her on the tip of her nose. "Wherever we are, as long as we're together, is home to me, but we don't have to give up the apartment. In fact, the landlord hinted that he wants me to buy it."

"Really?" Caroline murmured, then draped her arms around my neck. "Let's do it. I love you so much, Maria. You know I'd follow you to the ends of the earth, don't you?"

"And I love you even more, Caroline Frank-Wagner. You're my reason for waking up in the morning, and the thought of you not being in my arms at night fills me with dread. Promise me you'll always stay by my side." I murmured, then noticed her heart pounding faster against my chest. Then a sliver of moonlight illuminated Caroline's face. A single tear slid down her cheek.

"Always, Maria. I promise."

———

I hope you enjoyed Maria and Caroline's love story. The following is an excerpt from the novel The Promise, which is available at all major online retailers.

"Are you scared? You know, enlisting in the marines?" Ashley asked, tightening her grip on my hand as we strolled around Lake Johnson. I stopped in my tracks and turned to face her, our eyes locking.

"What do you think?" I sighed, then she pulled me into her chest and kissed the tip of my nose. "I'm not scared of joining the service, Ashley. Losing you forever is my deepest fear."

Ashley's soft curves trembled, and I felt her heart beating against mine as our hug deepened.

Ashley had been my first at just about everything. For the last two years of high school we'd been inseparable, unable to be apart for any stretch of time. The thin, gorgeous eighteen-year-old had stolen my heart at the beginning of our junior year, and the night we graduated we'd skipped the parties and headed to her family's beach house on the outer banks. There we shared our true feelings for the first time, both with words and our bodies.

"I love you so much, Carly." Ashley's velvety voice trembled, and her grip on me grew stronger. "How am I going to survive without you?"

A tear slid down my cheek, because the same fear filled me with an ache I'd never experienced before. I felt Ashley's fingers on the back of my neck, and seconds later, she was staring into my eyes again.

"Let's run away." I whispered, the sound of frogs and cicadas nearly drowning out my voice.

The pressure behind my eyes burned, because I wanted nothing more than to be by her side, always. Her thumb swiped at the tears now flowing down my cheeks. Ashley's full lips inched closer to my mouth, and seconds later her lips crashed against mine, taking my breath away. Searing heat surged through me, and my legs trembled as I tried to maintain my balance. My friends had all complained about having sex with their boyfriends, how all the hype around their first time had only led to disappointment and guilt.

Making love to Ashley was different, and not just because we were both girls. We'd been each other's first, and the emotional and physical bond between us had only deepened with every encounter. The feel of her silky skin was intoxicating, and combined with the love I felt, I couldn't imagine ever being with another woman.

There had been many sleepless nights where I lay awake, wondering what it would be like to live with Ashley, and to wake up in her arms every morning. She was my everything.

"Please," I moaned, breaking the kiss, "you know I want to be with you, more than anything else in the world."

"Then let's do it. Between our savings and graduation gifts we can afford to strike out on our own." Ashley's voice cracked. I placed my hands against her shoulders and gently pushed her away.

"You know we can't do that." I sniffed, then backed out of her arms and began pacing, hugging myself. "Not that I don't want to, but..."

"I can still go to college." Ashley interrupted. "We couldn't afford Harvard medical school, but we..."

"I have to join the service. And as much as I care for you, Ashley, being a surgeon has been your lifelong dream. Graduating from Harvard would open up almost any door for you." Without thinking, I placed a lock of my chestnut hair in my mouth, a habit I'd broken in elementary school.

Ashley abruptly turned away and stalked a few feet ahead. That was when I noticed her shoulders shaking, and my resolve threatened to break. As much as she wanted to be a doctor, how could I let go of this love so soon? I sighed, then picked up a stone from the path and skimmed it across the water.

"Damn it," I whispered. "Why do we have to choose?"

"I'm sorry," Ashley murmured. "I shouldn't be pressuring you like this. You're heading to San Diego for basic training in three days, and I'm off to Florida tomorrow. You have your whole life ahead of you, and so do I." She sighed, then wrapped her arm around my waist and we both stared across the lake. I could hear honking in the distance, and moments later a flock of geese descended. They'd always frightened me, especially when they defended their nests. But that fear didn't even come close to the terror I felt now at losing Ashley.

"Does it really have to end?" Ashley murmured. "Can't we..."

"I don't want it to, Ashley. But my parents want me to serve four years in the marines, and then Dad wants me to join the family business. You know, that's where my parents met, in the service. Shit." I muttered, stepping away and kicking a stone into the water, provoking a flutter of wings from the geese now swimming a few feet away.

"And I'll be in med school. Never-ending school." Ashley sighed, both of us dreading our new lives, yet excited to start it. "We can't… we just can't make it, not with all these obstacles in front of us. Long distance relationships always fail."

I strolled over to where Ashley stood, and placed my hands on her forearms. "You are my first love, Ashley, and no one will ever take that away from me."

Her blue eyes were wet, and she glanced up to the darkening sky, and gulped. "Let's make a promise."

My breath hitched, and I nodded for her to continue.

"Both of us have a bunch of things happening to us over the next few years, so yeah, a long-distance relationship isn't going to…" Ashley turned her head and swiped at her eyes, then met my gaze again. "In ten years' time, if we both are still single, let's meet at our high school reunion and maybe we can…"

"Pick up from where we're leaving it now?" I whispered, a flicker of hope radiating throughout my chest. Then, it dawned on me that the likelihood of that happening was close to zero.

Ashley nodded, her face softening while her cheeks burned red. It felt like someone had punched me in the stomach, and I'd do anything in the world to see Ashley's teeth split into a smile.

"I promise you, Ashley, in ten years we will be together, though I don't know how I'm going to wait so long."

"This isn't over, Carly, and it never will be. I promise you will always have my heart, and if I have to wait until…"

"Stop." I reached up and laid a finger across her full lips. "I can't bear this anymore." A sob threatened, and I didn't want to make our goodbye more painful than it was.

"I love you, Carly." Ashley kissed the tip of my finger, then brushed her lips across mine.

"Oh Ashley, I love you too." I whispered, then we both turned toward the lake and watched the water turn orange from the setting sun. "Don't you ever forget that."

About the Author

Tessa Vidal is a church secretary by day, and at night she tells stories of women falling in love.

Milton Keynes UK
Ingram Content Group UK Ltd.
UKHW020641310723
426074UK00019B/1397